I am a
GENIUS of
UNSPEAKABLE
EVIL and I want
to be your
CLASS
PRESIDENT

JOSH LIEB

razOr
bill

An Imprint of Penguin Group (USA) Inc.

I Am a Genius of Unspeakable Evil and I Want to Be Your Class President

RAZORBILL

Published by the Penguin Group
Penguin Young Readers Group
345 Hudson Street, New York, New York 10014, U.S.A.
Penguin Group (USA) Inc., 375 Hudson Street, New York, New York 10014, U.S.A.
Penguin Group (Canada), 90 Eglinton Avenue East, Suite 700, Toronto, Ontario, Canada M4P 2Y3
(a division of Pearson Penguin Canada Inc.)
Penguin Books Ltd, 80 Strand, London WC2R 0RL, England
Penguin Ireland, 25 St Stephen's Green, Dublin 2, Ireland (a division of Penguin Books Ltd)
Penguin Group (Australia), 250 Camberwell Road, Camberwell, Victoria 3124, Australia
(a division of Pearson Australia Group Pty Ltd)
Penguin Books India Pvt Ltd, 11 Community Centre, Panchsheel Park, New Delhi – 110 017, India
Penguin Group (NZ), 67 Apollo Drive, Rosedale, North Shore 0632, New Zealand
(a division of Pearson New Zealand Ltd.)
Penguin Books (South Africa) (Pty) Ltd, 24 Sturdee Avenue, Rosebank, Johannesburg 2196, South Africa

Penguin Books Ltd, Registered Offices: 80 Strand, London WC2R 0RL, England

10 9 8 7 6 5 4 3 2 1

Copyright © 2009 The Great Josh Lieb Productions

Library of Congress Cataloging-in-Publication Data

Lieb, Josh

I am a genius of unspeakable evil and I want to be your class president / by Josh Lieb.
p. cm.

Summary: Omaha, Nebraska, twelve-year-old Oliver Watson has everyone convinced that he is
extremely stupid and lazy, but he is actually a very wealthy, evil genius, and when he
decides to run for seventh-grade class president, nothing will stand in his way.

Razorbill hardcover ISBN: 9781595142405
Razorbill paperback ISBN: 9781595143549

1. Genius—Fiction. 2. Identity—Fiction. 3. Politics, Practical—Fiction. 4. Schools—Fiction.
5. Family life—Nebraska--Fiction. 6. Omaha (Neb.)—Fiction. 7. Humorous stories.] I. Title.

PZ7.L61626 Im 2009

[Fic] 22

2008039692

Printed in the United States of America

For B., the nicest genius I know

Chapter 1:
FEAR ME

Someday you will beg for the honor of licking my feet. You will get down on your stupid, worthless knees and beg, "Please, sir! Please! Let me lick the diseased dog dung from between your toes." (I will be standing barefoot in the dung of diseased dogs—just to make it grosser for you.) And if I am in a good mood and am not too disgusted by your stupid, wormy tears or your stupid, scrunched-up face, I will allow you the signal honor of licking my feet clean. Even though you don't deserve it.

But that's all in the future. At the moment, I'm in the seventh grade.

In fact, at this *precise* moment, I am in Mr. Moorhead's English class as he prattles on about *Fahrenheit 451*. Moorhead considers himself a "cool" teacher (*see plate 1*). That means he still wears the clothes he wore in college. Unfortunately for Moorhead, college was ten years and twenty pounds ago. His legs look like a pair of light-blue water balloons, stuffed as they are into too-tight jeans. He can't get all the buttons on his crotch to

PLATE 1: Moorhead considers himself a "cool" teacher.

stay fastened anymore (*Way cool, Mr. M!*), and he wears plaid flannel shirts that gape open over his salmon-pink belly. He's balding, but he thinks if he leaves his hair messy enough, we won't notice. He also keeps a pack of cigarettes in the pocket over his heart. This is supposed to say, "I am a teacher, but I'm not a saint." In reality, it just makes his saggy man-breasts look bigger. It also says, "I smell bad."[1]

Moorhead is one of those sad people who go into teaching so they can be worshipped by the only people sadder than they are—students. Prime example: Pammy Quattlebaum, so-called smart girl and insufferable butt-lick, who sits in the front row, nodding her massive head frequently to show Moorhead that not only has she done the reading, she understands *exactly* what he's saying.

Meanwhile, I am in the back of the room, drawing pictures of bunny rabbits on my binder.

Moorhead is way too cool to lecture standing up or sitting down. Instead, he lounges sexily against his desk, elbow propped on the dictionary, as he lays his knowledge on us. "The book depicts a world turned upside down." (Pammy nods.) "A world where firemen don't put out fires—they set them." (Pammy nods again, more emphatically.) "A world where the most dangerous weapon you can own"—here he holds up his copy of

---

1. Which he does.

7

Fahrenheit 451—"is a book." (Pammy nods so hard I can hear her tiny brain rattle, like a popcorn kernel in a jelly jar.)

Moorhead, simulating deep thought, runs his fingers through the pubic growth that decorates his scalp. "What do you think? Are books dangerous? Are they... *powerful*?"

Pammy surges out of her seat, arm straining for the sky. She will apparently pee herself if she's not allowed to answer this question.

But Moorhead's eyes slide over to me. "What do you think, Oliver?"

Pammy shoots me a dirty look. Some of my other class-mates giggle and don't bother trying to hide it. Randy Sparks, the Most Pathetic Boy in School, stops licking dried peanut butter off his glasses long enough to give me a sympathetic smile.

Moorhead grins like he's made a great joke. I am fairly cer-tain I was only assigned to this class—which is far beyond my tested reading level—so he'd have someone to make fun of (besides Randy, of course).

I make him say my name again before I answer, "I don't know."

Moorhead's face crumples with disappointment, but his eyes shine with satisfaction. "Oliver. Didn't you do the reading?"

I shake my head sadly. Moorhead sighs. He looks like he wants to cry for me. Or burst out laughing. It's like his brain can't decide.

Actually, I read the book when I was two. And even *then* I knew it was regurgitated bird pap, fit only for morons and seventh graders. In case you're lucky enough to have escaped it, *Fahrenheit 451* is one of those books that is about how *amazing* books are and how *wonderful* the people who *write* books are. Writers love writing books like this, and for some reason, we let them get away with it. It's like someone producing a TV show called *TV Shows Are the Best and the People Who Make Them Are Geniuses.*[2]

In *Fahrenheit 451*, books are illegal (because they're so powerful) and a fireman's job is to burn all the books he can find in big bonfires. This is supposed to blow your freaking mind.[3]

Moorhead walks back to my lonely little desk and puts a comforting hand on my shoulder. "It's too bad you skipped

---

2. Probably the name of Aaron Sorkin's next project. Ha.

3. I plan on having a *Fahrenheit 451* party one day. To get in, you have to bring a copy of *Fahrenheit 451*. Then we build a big fire and . . . well, you do the math.

it, big guy. Because it happens to be one of the best books written in the past century."

His furry fingers rest on my shoulder like caterpillars. I decide not to bite them. One of the best books of the century? *Fahrenheit 451* doesn't rank as one of the best birdcage liners of the century.

And besides—even if it were "*one* of the best books". . . is that anything to brag about? Wouldn't it look kind of drab and shabby when compared to the book that's the actual best?

It doesn't pay to be good at something unless you are the absolute best at it. Otherwise, you'll eventually go up against someone who can beat you. That is why I do not try to play soccer, sing in the school chorus, or dance, even though I am moderately talented at all of these things. I concentrate on what I am good at: being a genius.

I am the greatest genius in the universe. I am the greatest genius in the history of the universe. Plus, I am unceasingly, unreservedly, unspeakably evil. Making me *the most powerful force for evil ever created*.

And poor Mr. Moorhead thinks I'm the dumbest boy in his English class.

The bell rings. Moorhead gives me one last pitying glance, then strolls back to the board. "Read the next chapter for tomorrow, people. And remember—nominations for student council have to be submitted at your next homeroom." He smiles at Jack Chapman, who lowers his handsome head modestly and runs a bashful hand through his soft and kinky hair. Jack exits with the throng, enduring much backslapping and people yelling, "You got my vote, Jack." I pretend to fumble with my books so I can see what happens next.

It's lunchtime. As always, Moorhead reaches into his shirt pocket for his pack of cigarettes and shakes one out. He does this right after class, even though he can't smoke in the classroom, even though he can't smoke in the school. He must walk a legally mandated ten yards off school property before he can smoke his death stick. But he always pulls it out right after class.

He looks at the cigarette with longing . . . then with surprise. He holds it close to his weak, middle-aged eyes. There's a message typed neatly on the little tube: YOUR DIET ISN'T WORKING.

Moorhead stares at the cigarette a moment, then looks up with suspicion and fury. But the only people he sees are me and Pammy, who is also dawdling, but for very different reasons.[4]

Pammy gives him a simpering smile, which he ignores.

---

4. She wants him to read a poem she wrote about lowering carbon emissions. Absolute garbage. Sample verse: *Carbon credits are the answer/ To our planet's dreaded cancer.*

I, near-retard that I am, am singing a song to myself as I look for my pencil under the desk. The only words to the song are *"Three, please. Can I see threeeee pretty pictures. . . ."* Moorhead gives me a scornful glance before hurrying out of the room.

But the look of terror on his face in that single, unguarded moment of surprise is truly a beautiful, beautiful thing.

There will be three full-color photographs of that moment waiting for me by the time I get to my locker.

Chapter 2:
CHILDREN ARE VERMIN

Let me explain children to you.

First off, I call them "children," not "kids." I am a child, and I am not ashamed to be one; time will cure this unfortunate condition. "Kid" is the cutesy name adults call children because they think "child" sounds too scientific and clinical. I refuse to call myself by their idiotic pet name. Your grandmother might call you "Snugglepants Lovebottom," but that's not how you introduce yourself to strangers.[5]

I also refuse to use terms like "teen," tween," and etc. I find them patronizing and putrid. They are fake words, used to disguise the truth—that anyone under the age of eighteen is legally (and that's the only thing that matters) a child.

As long as a person is a child, he cannot own property, conduct business, have a real job, or do anything of actual

---

5. Unless you have deep-seated psychological problems. Or happen to be named "Snugglepants Lovebottom"—in which case, you have my sympathy.

importance. There's a good reason for this: Children are loud, stupid, lazy, and ugly (*see plate 2*).

When they are not laughing (too loud and for no reason), they are screaming (too loud and for no reason). And when they're not doing either of those things, they're whining (too loud and for no reason). I would say they're like monkeys, but monkeys are cute.

I am reminded of a winter afternoon several years ago. Setting: a shadow-filled living room, illuminated by warm lamplight and the flickering of the television set. I was sitting on the floor, playing gin rummy with my mother (and letting her win, naturally). My dog Lollipop was curled up behind me, acting as a natural backrest. My favorite movie, *The Third Man*, was on TV. The Ferris wheel scene was playing, and Orson Welles was giving his lovely speech in which he compares all the useless people on the ground to "dots"—and wonders if anyone would really care if one of those dots stopped moving.

All was perfect... except, of course, for my father. "Daddy"[6] was sitting in his armchair, impatiently rattling the magazine he was reading, crossing and uncrossing his legs, breathing heavily. This is the way weak men signal that they are unhappy. He wanted to watch a political debate or a folk-music concert or a

---

6. He hates it when I call him that.

PLATE 2: Children are loud, stupid, lazy, and ugly.

news show—something stupid—but I shrieked when he tried to change the channel.

My mother said, "Little Sugarplum likes this movie."

15

Daddy made a particularly ugly face: "Little Sugarplum doesn't *understand* this movie." I thought his tone of voice was uncalled for.

After a while, Daddy started staring out the window. His face softened. A little smile played on his lips. "That's really beautiful, man."[7]

When my mother asked him what was so beautiful (*man*), he pointed to a group of neighborhood children playing in the snow outside. They were engaged in all the traditional winter sports: shoving snow down each others' shirts; shoving snow down each others' pants; making each other eat snow.

Daddy was overcome by the charm of this scene. "They're just so amazing at that age. So innocent. So . . . pure. As pure as the snow they play in." He apparently hadn't noticed the places where the snow was distinctly yellow.

Then he remembered I was in the room. He turned and gave me a searching look. "Oliver . . . don't you want to go out and play with them? Make some new friends?"

Hmmm. Inside toasty and warm, with a pot of hot cocoa in easy reach? Or outside, wet and cold, catching diseases from a drippy-nosed scrum of screeching urchins?

---

7. Daddy is a bit of a hippie.

"No, Daddy," I said. "All the friends I want are right here."
And I gave his leg a great big hug. He winced.

But that was two years ago. Children are a problem that
continues to plague us, even today.

We can all agree that children are ugly. Their heads are
too big, their legs are too thin, their fingers too fat and
grasping—they are a complete mess. But what's most
shocking about them is that their greatest ugliness is on
the *inside*. I speak, of course, of their bigotry. I shouldn't
even have to mention this, because it is a natural extension
of their stupidity. Stupid people are bigoted because they
don't know any better. I am amused when goody-goodies
proclaim, from the safety of their armchairs, that children
are naturally prejudice-free, that they only learn to "hate"
from listening to bigoted adults. Nonsense. Tolerance is a
learned trait, like riding a bike or playing the piano. Those
of us who actually live among children, who see them in
their natural environment, know the truth: Left to their
own devices, children will gang up on and abuse anyone
who is even slightly different from the norm.

I happen to be slightly different from the norm.

Which explains why at this very moment, today, at two
minutes after two in the afternoon, Jordie Moscowitz is
blocking my path in the hallway.

"Excuse me, please," I say, meek as a mouse.

Jordie laughs.[8] He puts a hand on my chest. "I'd get out of your way, Chubby, but I don't think the hallway's wide enough for me to get past you!"

He says this very loudly, turning his head so a group of girls by the lockers can hear him. His mane of oily black curls jiggles around his greasy face. His mouth cracks in a crooked leer, exposing braces still coated with the scrambled eggs he had for breakfast. The girls giggle.[9]

Encouraged, Jordie opens his mouth to make another joke ...and then stops. His face goes slack. He suddenly looks tired, puzzled. Then his puzzlement turns to horror as a greasy fart *burps* out of the back of his jeans and fills the entire hallway with a smell like burning tennis shoes.

The girls shriek with laughter[10] and run screaming down the hall. Jordie watches them go, pathetically. Then he rubs his neck and walks away.

Jordie is new to this school—he only transferred in at the beginning of the semester. Otherwise he wouldn't have tried to pick on me. The other boys (and some of the bigger

---

8. Of course he does.

9. Of *course* they do.

10. *Of course they do.*

girls) learned a long time ago not to bully me, or else they'd end up feeling tired, weak, and thirsty. Even if they don't *know,* they know it, they know it. Experience has trained them. The little reptile brains inside their heads tell them, "Leave this one alone." So they do.

Two forces make this possible:

1) **LAZOPRIL**: A chemical I invented with my first home chemistry set.[11] It completely saps the hostility from anyone exposed to it and makes them feel like doing nothing more violent than taking a nap. Side effects include sudden intense flatulence (what scientists call farts) and roughly a three-month delay in the onset of puberty. That is to say—every time you're dosed, you put off your growth spurt by three months. I used to mix this stuff up without wearing gloves, which probably explains why my private parts are still as bare as a freshly plucked chicken.

2) **PISTOL, BARDOLPH, AND NYM**: My bodyguards. Not their real names, of course; these are code names I picked from a Shakespeare play I used to like.

It's their job to shoot a mini-dart full of Lazopril into the neck of anyone who tries to mess with me. They do other chores for me as well—like slipping the doctored pack of cigarettes into Moorhead's pocket, or printing

11. First grade.

up photographs from the two thousand hidden cameras I have scattered around the school[12] and putting them in my locker. I give them orders through the transmitter implanted in my lower jaw. I just *say* I want something to happen and it *happens*. It's like magic but much more expensive.

Obviously, there's more than three of them. There's a Pistol, Bardolph, and Nym who guard me when I'm at school; then there's a Pistol, Bardolph, and Nym who guard me after school. An entirely different trio is on duty when I sleep at night.

One of my corporations does all the hiring. I don't even know which of the people who surround me are my bodyguards; it's safer that way. If I'm attacked, I don't want to tip off my assailant by looking around for my bodyguards—which I would invariably do if I knew who my bodyguards were.

I do have my suspicions, however. One of my protectors is probably the heavily muscled Chinese exchange student who happens to be in all my classes. Nobody knows his name, he doesn't seem to speak English, and he shaves twice a day. And I'm curious about the new librarian who has a Marine Corps tattoo on her ankle.

---

12. No, I don't have any cameras in the bathrooms. Why would you even *think* such a thing? What's the matter with you?

They don't know I'm their employer. They just know that someone is paying them—and paying them very well—to protect the good-looking, slightly pudgy child at Gale Sayers Middle School and to do whatever he asks.

They're the only reason I can walk unmolested through the school hallways, among the throngs of thimble-brains and savages who call themselves my classmates. They're the reason no one even looks at me as I open my locker, even though—not three feet away—a gang of boys is giving Barry Huss, the shortest boy in school,[13] an atomic wedgie.

And these are the creatures my loving father, dear old Daddy, wants me to be friends with. Daddy wants me to be popular. To play team sports with these dimwits. To invite them over for sleepovers.

I'd rather have a sleepover with a flea-filled rabbit carcass.

---

13. In fifth grade, when he was the tallest boy in school, he was so stubborn he picked on me every day for a month. That was a stinky, stinky month for Barry Huss.

Chapter 3:
I AM INCONVENIENCED

They say that men inherit their brains from their mothers. This is false. My mother is a shapeless, witless mass of mousy hair, belly fat, and boobs. Don't get me wrong, I am very fond of her. (Do I love her? Am I capable of love? A question even I can't answer.) She is very useful for making grilled-cheese sandwiches and tucking me into bed. I like to make her smile, and I try to do that a lot.

Does that detract from my evil? No. Even Vlad the Impaler had a mother. My fondness for "Mom" (she likes to be called that) serves as a nice counterpoint to the general rottenness of my character.[14]

I'm heading home on the school bus now, which means Mom is currently in the kitchen making me a grilled cheese with pickle chips.

The hot sandwich that greets me when I get home is

---

14. Go look up "counterpoint" in the dictionary.

perhaps the highlight of my day. It's "A Small, Good Thing."[15] It's also, unfortunately, very fattening, and one of the reasons that, although I am very, very handsome, I am slightly over-round.

The bus ride home is a comforting prelude to that melted-cheese nirvana, with a soothing sound track that remains reliably the same every day: My fellow students shriek and gabble like baboons; Tippy, the stubble-faced bus driver grunts, "Knock it off," every thirty seconds; the helicopter thrums rhythmically overhead.

I sit on my bench. Fifth from the back, left side, alone. Always alone. That's one of the benefits of being me. The children who are my age or older think I'm a stupid freak. The children who are younger are scared of me. Either way, nobody wants to sit with the dummy.

It's spring, but there's still a nip in the air, so I reach under my bench and turn on the seat warmer. The on/off switch is disguised as a dried-up wad of bubble gum. If I twist the booger next to it, the bench will give my buttocks a gentle massage. Not the green booger, the yellow one. The green booger controls my air-purifying unit. But I won't need that today—I'm almost home.

Or so I think. The first sign of trouble is when the sub-

---

15. To quote the title of an awful short story. Why do people insist on ranking it among Carver's best work? It's a perfect showcase of everything that's wrong with his fiction.

human squealing of my classmates goes up an octave. The bus brakes to a grinding, unhappy halt. Somebody screams, "It's Sheldrake!" And that's that. A mad dash by everyone to squeeze onto one side of the bus (annoyingly, mine) so they can catch a glimpse of the great man.

Lionel Sheldrake is the third-richest man in the world, but he still lives here in Omaha. We actually have two billionaires in Omaha, which is far too many for a city this size. Everyone in town is excited to have such rich people living here. It's like they think being rich can rub off on them.

Sheldrake's even better than the other billionaire, though. For one thing, he's richer. For another, Sheldrake *looks* like a billionaire (*see plate 3*): tall, sharp-eyed, lean-cheeked, hawk-nosed. And he travels in style. What's stopped my bus is a Sheldrake motorcade: Two giant black armored SUVs, one in front and one behind Sheldrake's armored black Rolls-Royce. That's how Sheldrake travels. If Sheldrake were going to the 7-Eleven to buy a Big Gulp (which he wouldn't— he's too rich to run errands for himself), he would drive there in his Rolls, with SUVs full of bodyguards surrounding him. The third-richest man in the world needs to be safe.

The moment Sheldrake exits the Rolls, my classmates emit a collective gasp of awe, like a thousand tiny farts. The great man strides imperiously toward his destination—a small bank he owns—never once looking around him. His bodyguards surround him and clear his path. When he is

PLATE 3: Sheldrake looks like a billionaire: tall,
sharp-eyed, lean-cheeked, hawk-nosed. And he travels in style.

out of the road, the chief bodyguard waves us on—traffic may resume.

As we drive past the bank, Sheldrake looks back and gives the bus a small worried look.

"Jeez! Why's the seat so hot?!" says Stephen Turnipseed, who's forced himself next to me. I give him my winningest *let's be best friends forever* smile. He backs off. "Your butt radiates heat, man. Hey!" he yells, as he heads down the aisle. "Fatso's butt radiates heat!"

I let my lip quiver like I'm going to cry and stare out the window.[16]

"Home is the fisherman, home from the sea...." and home is Oliver as I enter the kitchen through the garage. My pretty dog Lollipop barks happily, then squats on the linoleum and squirts a little to show her subservience. Mom sits at the counter, chin propped in her hands, staring sadly at an overcooked grilled-cheese sandwich—burned-black bread and cold hard cheese. "It's ruined," she moans. The Sheldrake motorcade has made me late, throwing off Mom's delicate timing. I try to cheer her up by smacking my lips as I bite in, even though it tastes like I'm eating Elmer's glue slathered between charred rubber mouse pads.

---

16. Interesting fact: I actually *can't* cry; it's physically impossible. At least, I've never done it before. A hypothesis: My brain is too powerful to be overcome by simple animal emotions. This was very confusing for Mom when I was a baby, until I began faking it after a few weeks to make her happy.

I allow her to hug me, then I give her the feeble description of my school day that she finds so thrilling. ("It was fine. I got a D on my geometry quiz. Somebody puked in the library.") She laps it up,[17] chin still propped in hands, as she watches me consume my sandwich and tomato juice. Lollipop stands sentinel at my feet, waiting for me to drop something.

Descriptions are in order. Mom, as I've mentioned, is fat, bad-haired, big-breasted. She wears tentlike sweaters and corduroy skirts, which she buys at a store that hides in a dark corner of the mall, next to Hickory Farms. Her hair is long and stringy and tainted with ugly veins of natural gray.

Lollipop is another type of creature entirely. Long, lean, lithe, she is a pit bull mix who is very, very muscular and very, very striped. She has teeth like ivory daggers, legs like dappled stalactites, and eyelashes both more beautiful and more delicate than fairy wings (*see plate 4*).

Currently, I like my mother slightly more than I like my dog. Both Lollipop and Mom share a slavish devotion to me, and both tend to drool when they're happy. But Lollipop can't make grilled-cheese sandwiches.[18]

Mom is talking: ". . . and then I saw Mrs. Albers at the No Frills Supermarket. She was buying eggs and food-

17. The story, not the puke. Again, what's wrong with you?

18. Yet. I am working on that.

PLATE 4: Lollipop is another type of creature entirely. Long, lean, lithe, she is a pit bull mix who is very, very muscular and very, very striped. She has teeth like ivory daggers, legs like dappled stalactites, and eyelashes both more beautiful and more delicate than fairy wings.

coloring so she could make Easter eggs. She said Ferdinand is going to have some little friends over to roll them on the front lawn, and she was wondering if you wanted to come. Isn't that wonderful?"

Ferdinand Albers is five years younger than myself. He is morbidly obese, has bright red ears and yellow hair that smells like tuna salad. If I show up for his egg roll, I'll likely be the only "little friend" who does. Still, maybe I should go; it would be a good cover. And it would make Mom happy.

I think what's comforting about my mother is that she would love me even if I were as dumb as I pretend to be. She genuinely believes I am the boy who couldn't tie his own shoes until he was ten—and yet she still thinks the sun and moon revolve around me! Call it what you will—stupidity, hormones, self-delusion. I call it Mom.

Her devotion stands in stark contrast to some other parents I could name.

"And your father just called. He's going to be home early."

"Yippee for him," I say, perhaps a trifle unenthusiastically, and with maybe—*maybe*—a slight roll of my eyes.

That was a slip. Mom looks at me a little funny. There's a question on her lips. I save the situation by suddenly slapping my hands together like a seal and giving a moronic grin. "Yay, Daddy! Yay!" I dance in a little circle, hopping from foot to foot, with Lollipop barking at my heels. Mom smiles, all doubts erased. "Ollie loves Daddy!" I scream, like a brain-damaged baby, then I skip—*skip*—like a happy fairy in a shiny green forest, out of the kitchen with its peeling, urine-colored linoleum floor, down the hallway with its turdly brown carpeting, and into my room, with its *delightful* brown and yellow color scheme. Lollipop gambols happily beside me.

As soon as my bedroom door hisses shut behind me, the cretinous smile leaves my face. I walk past the shelves full of broken toys and ripped-up Archie comics, past the bed shaped like a race car and the posters of cute kittens, and reach for the framed photograph of my father shaking Ralph Nader's hand. I give the nail from which it hangs three swift tugs. Silently, the floor I'm standing on descends into the ground. The photograph and the kitten posters remain suspended above me as Lollipop and I are swiftly lowered through my house's foundation into the earth—ten feet . . . twenty feet . . . thirty. Finally my bedroom floor comes to rest at the center of an enormous concrete cavern, the length of ten football fields. Lionel Sheldrake is waiting for me there. He's on his knees.

"I'm so sorry," he says.

I rap his noble cheek with the back of my hand. "You made Mom sad."

Chapter 4:
BEHIND EVERY GREAT FORTUNE IS A CRIME

How does a twelve-year-old boy become the third-richest person on earth?

The easiest way is to inherit a bunch of money. Unfortunately, my parents are neither rich nor dead. I've been forced to rely on my genius, which, in all modesty, has made making money pretty darn easy. I've gone from small-scale investments in the stock market to large-scale manipulation of that same stock market to titanic-scaled feats of corporate piracy in just a few short years. I now own land in all fifty states and most of the capitalist countries of the world. I own investment banks, baseball teams, borax mines, and banana plantations. I own one movie studio, two television networks, and three newspaper syndicates. I own the tobacco company that makes Mr. Moorhead's cigarettes; he's literally *paying* me to kill him. How delicious is that?

All my businesses are scrupulously legal.[19] Not because I have any moral problems with crime. It just makes my life

---

19. Well, I cheat on my taxes a little.

easier to obey the law. Crime is for poor people; you don't need to rob the bank if you own it.

That said, my tender age is a problem. Strictly speaking, I'm not allowed to own or do anything. A twelve-year-old can't sign a contract or negotiate a deal with a third-world dictator. I have to hide my age and identity behind a screen of shell corporations, limited partnerships, and holding companies. And I need a figurehead—a patsy—to be the putative leader of this financial juggernaut.

Which is why Lionel Sheldrake is quivering at my feet. "Get up, Sheldrake," I bark gently, "and walk with me."

Sheldrake is the cornerstone of my cover. Cover is deception. Cover is why I pretend to be stupid when I'm not. Cover is why magicians' assistants are always beautiful—so they can distract you while the magician takes a peek at your card. Cover is safety.

One of my minions throws a silk cape over my shoulders—it gets chilly this far underground. The cape is purple, to match the color of the walls. The color of royalty. Sheldrake and I stroll through the massive cavern. Above us, in an iron web of scaffolding, technicians in white lab coats build and test prototypes of my latest inventions. On either side of us, less-skilled "worker" minions dressed in red jumpsuits drive carts in and out of the tunnels that lead to some of my skyscrapers, warehouses, helipads, and airstrips.[20] This is the nerve center of my Empire. I started building it two years ago, and completed it last summer during a two-week vacation in Hawaii. Daddy thought he won the trip in a raffle; in reality, I needed my parents out of the house while my workmen excavated beneath it.

Sheldrake is babbling an excuse. A meeting he was in ran late, which is why his motorcade was running late, which is why my bus was delayed, which is why Mom burned my sandwich. I'm not in the mood for his whining: "You should have left the meeting at the scheduled time," I murmur darkly.

"But I was talking to the *president.* He'd traveled halfway across the country to see me. I couldn't just walk out," he sputters.

"You're Lionel Sheldrake. You can do whatever you want."

Sheldrake doesn't always grasp just how important my money has made him. In private, he may be my cringing lackey. But to the rest of the world, he is a god.

Five years ago, I stole twenty dollars from my mother's purse. This is the great crime my fortune is based on.

---

20. I even have a submarine base on the Missouri River. Just in case I want to blow up Iowa or something.

I used the money to play bingo with my grandmother in a church basement. I'd noticed on previous bingo trips with Granny that certain letters and numbers came out of the hopper more often than others; I suppose it was the shape of the Ping-Pong balls they were written on. Equipped with that knowledge, I picked bingo cards that were likely to win—and went home five hundred dollars richer.[21]

I turned this money into a certified check, which I used to start an online stock-trading account. The rest is history. Unfortunately, after I made my first million, certain people got curious—the Internal Revenue Service, specifically. I knew I needed some cover.

So I went looking for some.

My second-grade teacher Mrs. Guerra used to joke that I was so stupid I could get lost on my way back from the bathroom.[22] In reality, the reason I used to wander away from school so often was that I was looking for cover. I found it, strangely enough, outside the same church basement where I'd won my bingo money. An Alcoholics Anonymous meeting was letting out, and the lost souls were congregating on the sidewalk. One of them caught my attention immediately.

---

21. I paid Granny a hundred bucks not to tell my parents I'd won. They'd have made me put the money in a bank.

22. I have a tape of her saying this. I also have a tape of her crying when my finance company repossessed her Corvette.

AA is a great resource for finding cover agents. Many of these creatures come from impressive backgrounds and have done great things in the past—but they've all been humbled by their addiction to booze. Once they're clean, they are frequently desperate to redeem themselves in the eyes of the world.

When I first saw Lionel Sheldrake, he had been sober for ninety-three days and smelled like an overcooked lamb chop (*see plate 5*). I was immediately impressed by his bone structure and trim figure—he would clean up well. His clothing was old but of good quality; Brooks Brothers, from the look of it. So I climbed out of the garbage can I was spying on him from and asked the nice man if he would help a lost little boy find his was back to school. The nice man said yes.

During our walk, I asked him a lot of stupid questions, like children do, and quickly learned his name; it had a nice patrician ring. And I liked his accent—he spoke with the clipped vowels you hear in the New England prep school elite. I decided I'd found my man. As he said goodbye to me on the school steps, I slipped five thousand dollars into his hand. "Get yourself a new suit and a haircut," I told him, "and meet me outside the church at noon tomorrow." He blinked, then stared at the money with wide, frightened eyes—he acted as if a butterfly had just crapped an emerald into his hand. I reached out my pudgy little paw and curled his fingers

PLATE 5: When I first saw Lionel Sheldrake, he had been sober for ninety-three days and smelled like an overcooked lamb chop.

around the cash: "There's plenty more where that came from."[23] Then I walked into school.

He was an hour late the next day, and when he did show up, he was drunk. I couldn't really blame him for that. Seven-year-olds who hand out five-thousand–dollar tips are unusual. He told me later that I'd spooked him so badly, he'd sworn not to come back, but curiosity and greed had gotten the better of him. I was glad. A little research on the Internet had taught me that Lionel Sheldrake, recovering alcoholic with an apartment on skid row, used to be Lionel Sheldrake, hotshot insurance executive with a house in Happy Hollow. Then he'd started drinking and lost it all. He was a native of a good Connecticut suburb and a graduate of Cornell University. His ancestors came over on the *Mayflower*—all that junk that looks good in the newspaper. I'd chosen well.

I got him a haircut. I bought him a suit. I made him sign a few contracts. And before long, people were saying that Lionel Sheldrake was an *important*[24] man.

Actually, he's a whiny man, and I'm getting tired of his excuses. "Beefheart," I bark, as Sheldrake prattles on. Somewhere in the depths of the control center, one of my minions hears me and obeys my command. The sweet dis-

---

23. It was actually more like, "There's pwenty more where that came fwom." I had the *cutest* little speech impediment back then.

24. i.e., rich.

cordant notes of my favorite song, "Adaptor," by Captain Beefheart and His Magic Band immediately fill the room at an ear-shattering volume, drowning out Sheldrake completely. My face relaxes into a smile. Nobody understands me like the Captain.

And then I frown. Because an automated warning voice has risen over the music. In flat, robotic tones, it repeats, over and over again: "Daddy's home. Daddy's home. Daddy's home."

Chapter 5:
MY DOG LOLLIPOP

According to the fortune-cookie logic most people live by, the best things in life are free. That's crap. I have a gold-plated robot that scratches the exact part of my back where my hands can't reach, and it certainly wasn't free.

But the best things in life *can* be cheap. My dog Lollipop cost only fifty-three dollars in adoption fees at the animal shelter. I found her there when she was three months old. She was a pudgy dewdrop of brindled fur and baby teeth, smiling happily at the world from a cold and barren cage. Her tail flicked back and forth like a windshield wiper through a puddle of her own pee. Apparently, she had to be kept apart from the other dogs because they picked on her. Idiots.

Daddy didn't like her, either. He kept trying to steer me to something "cuter." But I knew she was my dog the second she lunged at the bars of her cage and tried to bite his stupid face off.

When my dog Lollipop was five months old, she ran away. I don't think Daddy was sorry to see her go. Lolli had all these precious habits, like chewing up his man-sandals and peeing on his briefcase. One time, she made a poo on his favorite chair that looked almost exactly like a little brown dog. She's a very talented girl!

Mom tried to cheer me up by making me an ice-cream sundae every night. Actually, I was only pretending to be sad.[25] Lolli hadn't really run away. I'd sent her to a secret dog-training facility in the Basque region of Spain.

The Basque are an ancient people famous for wearing little hats and drinking wine in great curving spouts from leather canteens (*see plate 6*). They provide local color in the works of Ernest Hemingway. Since time began, apparently, they have lived in what is now southwest France and northern Spain.

Generally, you trace the ancestry of a people by looking at their language. Even if we didn't have history books to tell us, we'd know that Americans come from England, Africa, and everywhere else because the language we speak has words from England, Africa, and everywhere else.

We don't know anything of the sort about the Basque. Their language is an absolute mystery, completely unrelated to the French and Spanish gabble around them. We don't know where they came from, originally. Did their ancestors arrive in Basque country on ships from ancient

---

25. I ate the ice cream anyway.

PLATE 6: The Basque are an ancient people famous for wearing little hats and drinking wine in great curving spouts from leather canteens.

Egypt? Did they travel overland from Finland? There's just no telling.

A consequence of speaking such a strange language is that almost no one understands a word they're saying.

Daddy was a little surprised to discover Lolli, perfectly healthy, sitting in our driveway one afternoon about two months after she ran away. He was even more surprised to discover she was now house-trained, could be walked without a leash, and fetched the newspaper every morning.

He would be outright blown away if he knew some of the other tricks she'd learned. Only I know about those, and only I know the Basque commands that make her do them:

Gelditu = "Stay."
Eseri = "Sit."
Hil = "Kill."
Hil Ito = "Kill but make it look like an accidental drowning."
Garbitu = "Clean up your own poops in a plastic bag."[26]

That's just a sample. She has over eighty commands in her vocabulary.[27] Naturally, everyone who hears me thinks I'm just speaking some childhood nonsense language to my dog. My only worry is if I run into a Basque speaker in Omaha. And that is not likely.

Lollipop is sitting at Daddy's feet right now, staring up at him as he eats his dinner. She always sits there. Waiting. Not waiting for him to drop some food (he won't). Waiting

---

26. A surprisingly difficult trick. It was much easier for her to learn how to load and fire an armor-piercing missile.

27. Plus over a dozen nonverbal commands. Maybe *your* vocabulary will be that big someday!

for something bigger. Like a cobra watching a zookeeper, waiting for him to look away for *just* a second. . . .

Daddy tries to ignore her, but I notice he always keeps a firm grip on his knife.

He's looking thoughtfully over his glasses as he cuts his ham steak into dainty bites and tells us about his amazing day.

"I told the man, 'Look, I'm flattered—it's a very generous offer. But it's really not for me. I'm needed where I am.'" He lowers his eyes modestly. Daddy is constantly lowering his eyes modestly. It's like he's scared he'll see all the people he thinks are admiring him.

"You did the right thing," gushes Mom. She's leaning forward on her elbows, eager not to miss a syllable. "You always do the right thing!" The poor dear really doesn't know any better.

To my thinking, the only "right thing" my father ever did was marry Mom. That happened about six months after their first date, during their senior year at the University of Nebraska. I have a picture of them on that date (*see plate 7*)—it was a dance of some sort. Mom is the beaming blonde head-cheerleader. Daddy lurks next to her, a frazzled, bowtied nerd, who somehow mustered the nerve to ask this fertility goddess out and still can't believe she

PLATE 7: I have a picture of them
on that date—it was a dance of some sort.

said yes. So they got married, I was born a few months later,[28] and the end result is I have to eat dinner with this man every night. That's at Mom's insistence, by the way. Daddy and I would both prefer to eat in our rooms.

But I should let him finish his story: "So then he tried to offer me even *more* money, which kind of confirmed for me that my head was in the right place. I mean, I didn't get into this business for the money."

That's for sure. Daddy runs the local public broadcasting affiliate. That's the television channel that runs *Sesame Street*. Do you like *Sesame Street*? Well, Daddy doesn't have anything to do with that. In fact, he thinks *Sesame Street* is "out of step with today's pre-tweens." But it's popular, so he has to keep it on his station.

Here's what Daddy really does: Sometimes when you turn on a public broadcasting station, you will see an obese overrated opera singer singing and sweating (but mostly sweating). These performances are interrupted every seven minutes by a couple of people who smile too much. It's usually a man with glasses and a woman whose teeth are too big for her mouth. Both of them look like they have very bad breath. Behind them, about twenty bored people sit at a table answering telephones.

---

28. Again, you do the math.

45

The man and woman ask you to please, please call the number on your screen and make a donation, so they can continue to bring you fine programs featuring fat sweaty opera singers.

Daddy's job is to arrange these fund-raising extravaganzas. Sometimes he even appears onscreen as the smiling man with glasses. Have you seen him? He's got a bony triangle for a face, a feathery "smart guy" mini-mullet tickling the back of his neck, and narrow, narrow shoulders that somehow bear the sins of this world.

So, though I mock him, I have to admit my father can do *one* thing I can't: beg.

I roll my mouth around a brussels sprout and swallow loudly. I give him my gravest little-boy-seeking-wisdom look: "But wouldn't you be able to buy Mom presents if you made more money?"

Daddy responds with his gentlest *haven't I taught you anything?* voice: "Some things are more important than money, Ollie."

"And I don't need any silly presents," says Mom. She grabs our hands. "I've got everything I want right here!"

"Exactly," says Daddy, as he slips his hand out of hers. "Your mother has everything she could possibly desire."

This is not strictly true. I know for a fact she wants a new dishwasher and a rather lavish new Easter bonnet. She's also fond of expensive chocolates and porcelain statues of baby animals. In fact, it's precisely so Daddy could buy her these things that I had one of my minions offer him a job today.[29]

But that was a miscalculation. Because one of the great perks of Daddy's job is that it allows him to turn down other, *better* jobs. Then he gets to feel completely righteous and upright, and brag about it at the dinner table—with the end result being that Mom congratulates him for keeping her deprived. My life is a torture chamber of ironies.

Someone has started a motorboat engine under the table. Daddy looks annoyed: "For God's sake, Ollie, do something about that dog."

I look down. The rumbling is coming from Lollipop. She glares with cold hatred at Daddy. Her tongue hangs out of her mouth like an animal she's just caught and killed. Maybe she didn't like the way he stopped holding hands with Mom. Or maybe she sensed that I didn't like it.

"*Galtzazpiko,*" I whisper. Instantly, Lolli stops growling and shambles out of the room. My father smiles like he's won a great victory. He won't be smiling so much when he finds

29. I can't arrange for her to win prizes in contests too often. It looks suspicious.

47

the present I just told Lolli to leave him in his underwear drawer.

"Who wants banana pudding?" asks Mom.

My father pats his belly and gets up. "No thank you, dear. I think we're all pretty full." He gives me a meaningful look. "*Right*, Oliver? We've all had *plenty* to eat."

I am too dumb to understand meaningful looks. "I'm still hungry," I tell him, even though I'm not. Daddy scowls and exits into the living room.

I eat three bowls of pudding without tasting them.

Chapter 6:
GIRLS CAN BE CRUEL

"What's the matter, dork? Don't you have any ambition?"

The speaker is Tatiana Lopez, Meanest Girl in School. The dork she's talking to is me. It's lunchtime, and I'm sitting in my traditional seat at my traditional table, chewing on my traditional fluffernutter sandwich. Tatiana stands across the table, leaning over me, pointing her spiteful little pink fingernails in my face. She's good at this. Her spine curves and her shoulders hunch forward, so that she seems to lean over everyone she talks to, even when her victim is standing, even though she's short. It's magical.

"Mudlark," I mutter. It's the codeword I use to tell Pistol, Bardolph, and Nym not to interfere. Tatiana doesn't scare me. Much.

"What was that, Butterball?"

"Leave him alone, Tati."

Speaker Number Two is Randy Sparks, the Most Pathetic

Boy in School. More pathetic than I am, even—and he's not doing it on purpose. Randy is one of those unfortunate types who are geeky without being smart. He's painfully scrawny, wears thick glasses, has greasy skin—but is a low-C-average student at best. Too nerdy to associate with the normals, too stupid to associate with the nerds, Randy is a nation unto himself. I mean, even Pammy Quattlebaum has friends, and she's a melon-headed suck-up who's only been at this school a year. They make her do their home-work, but still, they're *friends*.

Here's how pathetic Randy Sparks is: He chooses to sit at the same table as me. There are plenty of empty tables around the room, but he chooses to sit with me. I discourage him,[30] over and over again, but he keeps hanging around like a wad of toilet paper stuck to my shoe. Revolting. I predict a great future for him in the field of getting-a-dead-end-job-and-dying-alone-and-unmourned.

Tatiana ignores him and keeps her poisonous brown eyes pointed straight at me. "Know what your problem is, Jumbo? No ambition. Here I give you the perfect opportunity to be *president* of the whole stupid class, and you're too scared to even try. You make me sick," she says venomously.

"Uh-huh," I say retardedly.

"You got plenty of guts," she adds. "It's just they're only

_____

30. Usually by pretending to be scared of him. It's funnier that way.

the kind that jiggle around your middle." She snatches the sandwich from my hands, takes a long, savage bite, then tosses the twisted crust into my lap. It oozes peanut butter and marshmallow fluff, like a crushed bug.

Tatiana smirks and preens with feline satisfaction. She plucks up the collar of the pink cashmere sweater she won in a contest and saunters away. I watch her go through half-closed eyes. Ah, Tatiana. You vile, deceitful, mean-spirited little goddess. You will get what you deserve. Someday.[31]

"Don't let her get to you." Randy Sparks has walked over and has the presumption to give me a comforting pat on the back. I squeal with feigned pain, "Stop hitting me, Randy! It hurts!"

Randy looks at his hand, amazed by his own strength. "But I was just—"

"Child abuse! Child abuse!" I grab my lunch bag and sprint from the room. The laughter of the chimpanzees follows me out the door.

It's been an eventful day. The reason Tati's so mad at me is because of what happened in homeroom this morning. My

---

31. I actually bought the company where her mother works, several years ago, just so I could transfer her to another office in some barren, godless place, like Death Valley or San Diego. Then Tati would have to move far, far from here. I haven't gotten around to that yet.

homeroom teacher, Lucy Sokolov, was leading us through the process of nominating candidates for student council. Ms. Sokolov is an intelligent but scary woman. She looks like someone stretched a thin layer of Silly Putty over a skeleton and slapped a red wig on top. My Research Department tells me she wants to be a novelist, but the publishing houses always reject her masterpieces. Which makes her mean. She takes out her thwarted ambitions on her students.

After my more spineless classmates finished nominating each other for the more meaningless offices (secretary, treasurer), we got to the meat of the issue: nominations for class president. Naturally, five people nearly got into a fistfight in their eagerness to nominate Jack Chapman. Sokolov sorted that out, and the nomination was swiftly seconded. Then she asked Jack if he would accept the nomination.

Every neck in the room twisted toward Jack, the best student in school, the wide-shouldered (but gentle) king of recess. Ah, Jack! That high Shakespearean brow. That broad masculine nose. He stared thoughtfully at his hands. Then he stood, paused, and nodded.

I cannot describe this nod adequately. It was slow, impressive. It was the kind of nod Abraham Lincoln would give. It was the humble nod of a man who has not sought out a position of leadership but who will take on that dreaded responsibility if his community needs him. And it was suddenly understood by all that we *did* need him. Everyone in the room—Sokolov included—seemed to melt an inch in the presence of such magnificence.

Everyone, that is, but me and Tatiana. Obviously, I'm too stupid to recognize greatness. Tatiana's so mean she hates greatness when she sees it. Her hungry little arm snaked into the air, demanding Sokolov's attention.[32] Sokolov frowned, confused. "What do you want, Miss Lopez?"

Tati stood. Tight curls. Tiny teeth. Snub nose. Cinnamon skin. She opened her mouth and let out the words that would forever sully Jack Chapman's moment of glory: "I nominate Oliver Watson for president."

The class, to its credit, was for once too disgusted to laugh. Sokolov looked like she'd been slapped with a fish. Tati threw me a mean wink and flounced down into her seat.

Logan Michaels, a desperate and fat girl who occasionally functions as Tatiana's slave, dutifully seconded my nomination. *La Sokolova* turned to me. "Oliver," she said, with an expression on her face like she'd just bitten into a chocolate bar and found a toenail, "do you accept the nomination?"

I made her explain the question to me three times before I declined.

---

32. The first time I'd ever seen her raise her hand before speaking in class.

Later, Tati taunted me in the cafeteria and violated the sanctity of my fluffernutter. But you saw all that.

I have P.E. after lunch. More accurately, my *classmates* have P.E. after lunch—I have a note from a doctor that says I will suffer explosive diarrhea if I ever have to take part in P.E. Coach Anicito doesn't like it when people drip *sweat* on the gym floor; he doesn't make me participate.

He does, however, make me suit up in shorts, T-shirt, and sneakers, like everyone else. Plus, like all the other boys, I have to wear a legally mandated (but in my case, wholly unnecessary) jockstrap.[33]

Today, like always, I stand by the water fountain, watching my classmates exert themselves. The boys play kickball on one side of the gym; the girls play kickball on the other. Liz Twombley, the Most Popular Girl in School, kicks a dribbler off the inside of her foot. Her curly blonde hair (and everything else) bounces as she tries to beat the throw to first. Both games come to a halt as everyone watches her with a mixture of longing and awe. Liz, bless her great big stupid heart, doesn't notice.

I'm catching up on some business. I have a bud—a listening device—in my ear so I can talk to Sheldrake. "I really think we should consider buying more Kreelco stock," he

---

33. I don't mind; it feels like a little hug.

natters. "The company is solid and the price is at an all time low."

"Sell all our shares," I command.

A moment of silence. Then: "Oliver, normally I wouldn't argue, but—"

"I said, sell it."

"But I thought—"

"Don't *think*, Lionel," I say. "You'll hurt yourself."

I pause to take a sip of cold chocolate milk from the water fountain. I get that by pressing on an old mildew stain on the wall. If I press the spot right below the stain, the fountain spits out root beer. Sometimes I switch back and forth between the two while I'm drinking. It's like making a root beer float in my mouth.

I burp. "Trust me. We'll buy it all back next week at half the price."

I do most of my business through Sheldrake. For security reasons, only fifty-two of my most-trusted minions even know of my existence. The next tier down is a group of five hundred agents who think Sheldrake is the head of the vast criminal empire they work for. Then there are roughly a thousand agents, scattered around the world, who don't even know who they work for. That way, my enemies can't get any information from them if they're captured.

And that's just the *secret* side of my Empire. There are also several hundred thousand people whom Sheldrake Industries employs openly (and who think Lionel Sheldrake is their boss).

"Next on the agenda," I say. "Redecorating. Put in a call to Paris—"

I shut up as Josh Marcil trots off the court and pushes me aside so he can get to the water fountain. He doesn't know about any of my secret buttons, so he makes a face as he slurps up the warm dishwater that comes out. "Tastes funny," he says.

I smile and say, "I like it."

He flares his stubby little nose at me and says, "You would." Then he quite unnecessarily pushes me again as he runs back to the game. My head bumps the wall. That hurts a little. Josh is a loud boy, chubby, freckled, and sweaty. I watch him go back to his position in the "outfield."

"You were talking about Paris—" says Lionel.

"Just a second." I click my jaw, taking me off the private channel I use for talking to Sheldrake, and onto the channel I use for Pistol, Bardolph, and Nym.

"Josh Marcil," I say. "Stomach." Then I click back over to Sheldrake and turn my back to the game. "Now, I was saying—"

From behind me I hear the loud hollow *Spong*! of a red rubber ball hitting the belly of a middle-school boy—hard. Then the sound of a middle-school boy falling to the ground and moaning.[34] Coach Anicito is yelling at someone: "No! We do *not* throw the ball at people on our team. Unacceptable!"

"As for Paris, Lionel," I say, through a cute little smile, "I think it's time we stopped playing games."

---

34. Don't be such a baby. He just got the breath knocked out of him.

Chapter 7:
WHAT USE IS A NEWBORN BABY?

Your earliest memory is probably of a walk in the park when you were four. Or getting a teddy bear for Christmas when you were three.

I can remember being born.[35] *Everything* about being born. What I saw. What I felt. What I heard. What I smelled.

I would give up half my fortune to forget that smell.

I was taken home the next day by two animals. One was big and soft and sloppy. She stared at me so much I was half convinced she wanted to eat me. The other animal was thin and rat-faced. He smiled when he looked at me. That was the first fake smile I ever saw.

Later that afternoon, while Mom (as I learned to call her) took a well-deserved nap, Daddy stood over me as I lay in my crib. He was talking to his college roommate on the phone.[36]

---

35. Actually, my memory goes back a little farther than that. I can remember the royal-purple walls of my mother's womb. Beautiful.

36. I had learned to understand English by listening to the nurses at the hospital. Some Spanish, too.

"Yeah, we named him Oliver Junior . . ." He listened for a second, then laughed like a machine gun going off—*ga-ga-ga-ga-ga*. "Of course, he's named after me, you jerk! Seriously, Don, you're *hilarious*."

Daddy settled into a chair and propped his feet on my changing table. "Oh yeah. I'm totally thrilled. You know, childhood and innocence—it's all very important to me. In some ways, I'm just a big kid myself, right?" He reached into my crib—for a second, I thought he was going to pet me—and grabbed a teddy bear, which he started squeezing absentmindedly.

"I can just *relate* to kids. I know how they think. Little Oliver Junior—the little guy's brain is so simple and pure and innocent, free from the prejudices of the ugly adult world." He looked in the mirror and started fiddling with his hair. "I'm looking at him right now, and it's like I'm looking at the future."

He suddenly froze. I focused my day-old eyes and saw that he'd found a gray hair buried in his brown mane. He rolled it between his fingers like it was a poisonous worm, then plucked it out savagely. Then he looked at himself in the mirror again. He was frowning now. I could hear Don nattering through the phone line, but it didn't look like Daddy was listening anymore.

"What? Huh? Yeah, I'm here." He lowered his voice and glanced at the door that led to where Mom was sleeping. "Listen, man . . . you know I couldn't be happier about bringing this fresh new life into the world. . . . But . . . I mean, *man*! It's all happened so *fast*. First Marlene, now a baby . . . I can't help wondering if maybe it all isn't gonna keep me from doing . . . well, the great work I'm *destined* for. . . ."

My crib was in a room that doubled as my father's home office. This was in our old apartment. The room was the size of a large closet, and the walls were painted a manly dark green, but Mom had plastered stickers of frogs all over them for my benefit. Daddy's computer was next to my crib. The only "great work" I ever saw him do on it was play backgammon.[37]

"You know, I feel like I'm destined to help all the children of the world, to be famous for it, right? Like, maybe I'll write a book or something. Or go on TV. And I wonder if it's *selfish* of me to devote so much energy to this *one* kid, when I could help so many. Like it's a distraction. . . ."

He listened for a second.

"No . . . he doesn't cry or anything like that. He just stares at you . . . like, he's always *staring* . . . with these big blank eyes. . . . And his forehead is, like, *huge*. Plus, his nose is almost *nonexistent*—just a flat spot in the middle of his face. . . ."

---

37. I soon put that computer to much better use.

He suddenly realized how that sounded. "Don't take that the wrong way. The kid's gorgeous. I'm looking at the little guy right now. He's . . . amazing, man."

For the record, he was still looking in the mirror when he said that.

"But, you know, what if . . . and it's way too early to tell, obviously, but what if he inherits *her* intelligence? I don't know if I could handle—no, *of course* I love her, man. That's not the point."

"I mean, she put on a little weight during the pregnancy, but I'm sure that'll come right off. . . ."

He sighed, the sigh of a man who suffers more than the world will ever know or care. It was a sound I would come to know well.

"I'm just saying . . . I've known since I was a kid that I was destined to produce something *amazing*. Something that would totally change the world. I don't know what—a book, a play, an invention—*something*. And I don't see how I'm going to do that with this instant family weighing me down."

Here Daddy looked at me. I smiled at him. It was the first fake smile I'd ever made.

It's interesting, on your second day of existence, to realize that your father is going to blame all the future failures of his life on you. Not an experience I recommend.

That was when I decided to "hide my light under a bushel"—to play dumb. I could already tell that Mom would be terrified by my brain. And Daddy . . . well, he didn't know it, but he already *had* produced "something amazing," something that would "change the world."

Namely, me.

But I didn't see any reason to share that information with him. I wasn't going to let him warm his frigid little heart by the hot flames of my genius.

If he couldn't love me for simply being what I appeared to be, he didn't deserve to know the greatness that lurked within. I resolved at that very moment never to care what Daddy thought, never to give him an inkling of what a magnificent monster he had sired. He meant nothing to me.

Nothing. Nada. Zilch. And I haven't, for one second, cared what he thought about me since.

P.S. All babies have little noses, you jackass.

Chapter 8:
I ACCEPT A CHALLENGE

Daddy sits at the head of the dinner table, toying with his beef stew, as he solves the world's problems for us. I'm not really listening, but the gist of his argument seems to be that we'd all be a lot better off with stricter seat belt laws. Mom listens with less than her usual rapt attention. She squiggles in her seat, which makes her cheeks jiggle, occasionally opening her mouth, as if to say something, then thinking better of it and closing her lips into a shy, delighted smile.

Daddy doesn't usually act like he cares much what Mom thinks, so it's fun to see how annoyed he gets when he doesn't command her full attention. "The simple lap belts of yore just won't do it anymore," he intones. "We've got to make people understand, these so-called classic cars need retrofits to conform to . . . is there something on your mind, Marlene?"

This last is said in a tone of controlled annoyance and (understandable) surprise that there would be *anything* on Mom's mind.

"Ollie was nominated for class president!" she explodes. "That pretty little Lopez girl nominated him. He said no, but they nominated him!"

He makes her repeat the news three times before he believes her.

I'd mentioned my nomination to Mom over my after-school grilled cheese (which was perfect, incidentally), but I'd had no idea it had made such an impact on her. I guess the excitement's been brewing inside her all afternoon, like a can of soda that's been shaken too much.

Daddy seems less impressed. "Oh," he says. "Well. Obviously some sort of—"

He stops himself before he says "joke." But I can hear it anyway. He awkwardly pats me on the head. "Congratulations, Oliver. That's . . . quite an honor." Then he starts buttering a piece of bread so he doesn't have to look at me anymore.

Mom trots off to the bathroom. Being the bearer of such momentous news has put an enormous strain on her bladder.

I lower my spoon and concentrate on my stew. Daddy and I don't talk much when we're alone. My mind relocates to my most pressing concern: a corrupt trade official in Hong Kong who's putting a serious crimp in my exports to South Asia. This will require a complex web of bribery to solve....

"Man. Student Council. That really takes me back."

I look up, surprised. Daddy's talking to me. Or, more accurately, he's talking to himself, and I happen to be in the room. He's leaning back in his chair, glasses off, eyes pointed at the ceiling as he casts his mind back to his glorious yesteryears.

"It was me. Rhena Vinson. Louis Goldberg. Heather Grich was secretary-treasurer one year. That's when you started to be able to tell. When we started to separate ourselves out. The people who were gonna make a *difference*, who felt a commitment to the community."

I don't think I've ever heard the planners of bake sales described in such glowing terms before.

"You know, we . . . It was like everybody suddenly realized that we were the ones who were going to do something important with our lives.[38] The whole class was saying, 'Okay, *you* guys represent us.' And when they made me president in tenth grade—I beat Louis by twenty-five

---

38. According to my Research Department: Rhena Vinson grew up to be a divorce lawyer in Fargo, North Dakota; Louis Goldberg is a massage therapist; Heather Grich was the most successful—she was president of a bank in Chicago. Then she had a nervous breakdown. She now works as a middle-school teacher.

votes—it was such an honor. I'd been given a trust, a sacred duty, and I knew I couldn't let them down."

I feel like I'm hearing the secret origin of the world's most annoying superhero. His eyes are moist. So are his lips. (Is he salivating?)

"It was just ... *amazing*, man ..."

Then, plainly all too soon, his reverie ends. He rubs his eyes and slips his glasses back on. He lowers his head and sees me.

More: He lowers his head and is *surprised* to see me.

Even more: He lowers his head and is *disappointed* to see me.

To see *me*.

And that's when I make up my mind.

He recovers his composure, shuffles the expression on his face, lands on something close to affection. He reaches out a tentative paw and gives me a weak pat on the shoulder. "But just getting nominated. That's great, too." He smiles at me. It is, by my calculation, the one-millionth fake smile he has ever foisted upon me—and one of the least convincing.

"Thanks, Daddy!" I beam back. "Thank you! Thank you!" I grab his wrist tight, kiss the back of his hand four times, five times, repeatedly, sloppily until he dares to pull it away. He looks a little scared as I turn my manic eyes downward and attack my stew.

I hate him.

I hate his pride. I hate his smugness. I hate his face.

I hate that there is something in his past that he values so highly. Something that is pure. When times are tough, when work is hard, when Daddy begins to doubt himself, he can always remember student council. He will always be the guy who beat Louis Goldberg by twenty-five votes. He will always be tenth-grade class president. And that makes him special. He thinks. It makes him better than me.

He thinks.

But I will ruin this for him. I will corrupt it. Just as he has corrupted so many of my finest hours. Just as he has ruined so many of my brightest days.

I will put a worm in his apple. I will make him pay.

Don't imagine I want his respect. His pride. His love. Because I don't. That's stupid. The very thought repulses me. I don't want him clasping me to his chest and saying,

"I'm proud of you, son." I'd rather die. I'd rather drink yak urine. I'd rather go on a carrot and cauliflower diet.

This is all about making him suffer. This is about me taking those golden, cherished memories of his student-council heyday and turning them into maggot-infested turd piles, great stinking wagonloads of crap and tears and bile. What once gave him pleasure to remember will now only remind him that he isn't so special after all. I will shame him.

His fat, selfish, stupid son is going to run for class president. And I am going to win.

It's going to be easy.

Chapter 9:
FAST AND BULBOUS

OBJECTIVE: Win the class presidency
TIME FRAME: One month
IMMEDIATE OBSTACLE: Getting on the ballot—contact Pinckney, Leon
LONG TERM OBSTACLES: Opponents—Chapman, Jack; Twombley, Elizabeth
ESTIMATED CHANCES OF SUCCESS: 100%

I scribble these notes to myself as Sheldrake natters on about radio revenue for the last quarter. "Ad sales were down three percent for our broadcast stations, and FCC fines were up," he worries nasally, through that magnificent patrician nose. "We may want to consider diversifying into the subscription satellite arena—"

"We already *are* diversified," I snap. "I own a controlling share of all North American satellite radio."

"Oh." Sheldrake looks through his papers. "When did that happen?"

"That day you stayed home sick with the flu."

Lollipop whimpers in the seat next to me and rests her massive head on my lap. I scratch her ears as I look out the window and down at the shining lights of my riverboat casinos below. Lollipop hates flying. I don't travel much as a rule—too risky—but tonight I had a lot to think about and a yearning to see the night sky, so I released a sleeping gas in my parents' bedroom and told Sheldrake to ready the blimp.

He looks a little green. I don't think he likes flying much, either—at least not in anything less technically advanced than a corporate jet. But I prefer the old-fashioned elegance of riding on the underside of a giant bag of helium. And the vibrations from the spinning propeller feel good (I have a tummy ache).

"Tell Research I want full probes done on Jack Chapman and Liz Twombley."

Sheldrake makes a note. "Who are they?"

"Classmates of mine."

He turns a shade greener. "You're ordering probes on *children*?"

I smile mischievously at him. "And what am I, Lionel? Chopped liver?"

Old jokes are wasted on Sheldrake. He merely nods and mumbles, "Sometimes I forget...."

We've moved past the river now and are circling over downtown Omaha. I can see the skyline, Rosenblatt Stadium, the classical elegance of Central High,[39] and the crystal dome that squats on the front lawn of the Mutual of Omaha Building. It delights me to look down at my city and know I own so much of it. And what I don't own I've tunneled under, infiltrated, compromised. This is how the pharaohs must have felt when they gazed at their pyramids in Giza—those gigantic pointy peaks jutting out of the sand like the humps of an enormous snake buried in the desert. A snake that would shake off the sand and *rise* someday at the pharaohs' command. That would slither out of the desert and bite the world on the butt.

But there's more to life than midnight blimp rides. I pull the speaking horn to my mouth and tell the captain to take us down.

Morning finds me trotting down the hallway before homeroom, on a quest to catch Principal Pinckney in his office.

Maybe *catch* isn't the right word. I know he's in there; I told Pistol, Bardolph, and Nym to make sure of that. Because I turned down the nomination when it was offered to me, I need Pinckney's approval to get on the ballot.

---

39. My father's alma mater, and the school I will someday attend.

Randy Sparks, the Most Pathetic Boy in School, stands by his locker, trying to scrub the sweat stains from the armpits of his T-shirt with an old toothbrush. All of Randy's shirts have horrible sweat stains—he lives with his dad, and his dad isn't very good at doing laundry. Plus, Randy sweats a lot. A lot of people—let's say, *everyone in the world but Randy Sparks*—would be trying to clean their shirt's armpits in the boys' bathroom, where the entire school couldn't see them. But bad things happen to Randy Sparks when he goes into the boys' bathroom. He doesn't have any bodyguards with Lazopril watching after him. I doubt he's taken a pee at school once in the last three years.

As I pass the teachers' lounge, the door opens and Mr. Moorhead backs out. He's clearly trying to slow the exit of my homeroom teacher, Ms. Sokolov, who just as clearly wants to get past him. She carries a dog-eared book under her arm; I squint to see the title—*Pnin* by Vladimir Nabokov. ". . . absolutely amazing," Moorhead gushes. "I mean, it really blew my mind." His traditional aura of sweat and smoke and stale coffee floods the immediate vicinity. It can't be healthy to smell so much like death this early in the morning.

"Mmm." Sokolov makes one final semi-polite noise, then slips past Moorhead to freedom. He watches her go, his eyebrows arched with lovesick yearning.

So Moorhead has a crush. Well, well, well...This could be an opportunity for real fun, in the screwing-with-peoples'-heads department. "Get me tape from Listening Post 2," I whisper. "Last half hour."

Principal Pinckney is still in his office when I get there, largely because some thoughtless custodian has blocked the door with two enormous boxes full of textbooks. I arrive just as he forces his way out, sending copies of *American History: A Glorious Feast* sliding across the glossy floor. He looks at them with annoyance, then at me with surprise. "What can I do for you, Oliver?"

"I want to be class president."

"I see," he says. He turns and kicks the nearest textbook so hard it bounces off three walls.

Leon Pinckney is a kindhearted, middle-aged ex-jock who is a more than competent science teacher. Unfortunately for him, his intelligence and large, expensive family have conspired to put him in the (marginally) more lucrative field of administration. And it's the job of administrators to tell half-witted little boys they can't be class president.

His chocolate-brown brow wrinkles with real sympathy as he tells me, "Uh...class president. You know, you have to get elected to do that...."

He smiles with relief when I explain the situation. He has an easy out. "I'm sorry, Oliver, but if you declined the nomination, there's really nothing I can do. It wouldn't be fair to the other kids if I made an exception, would it?"

He knows how much stupid children cherish fairness. I make a disappointed face and walk away, but I'm not particularly surprised. I knew it wouldn't be this simple. "Send in The Motivator," I whisper, as I make my way to homeroom.

Moorhead continues his discourse on *Fahrenheit 451*. I'm listening even less than usual—the conversation that's playing over my earbud is much more interesting. It stars Moorhead and Sokolov and was recorded in the teachers' lounge two hours earlier, just before I passed them in the hall.

MOORHEAD: (*fake surprise*) Oh, hey, Lucy! Fancy seeing you here (*lame giggle*)!
SOKOLOV: Oh. Hi . . . (*tries to remember his name*) Neil.
MOORHEAD: Can I pour you a cup of coffee?
SOKOLOV: No thanks. I don't drink coffee.
MOORHEAD: Smart. I'm on my third cup today (*lame giggle*).
SOKOLOV: That's too bad. Well, I'd really better get to class.
MOORHEAD: Oh! You're reading *Pnin*. That's by Nabokov, right?

Here I smile broadly. Not only is his flirting pathetic, he's also managed to mispronounce Nabokov's name. Normally excusable, but I know for a fact Sokolov wrote her master's thesis on that particular fat dead Russian genius.

SOKOLOV: Erm, yes. Wow, look at the time—
MOORHEAD: You know, I read *Pale Fire* in college. He wrote that, too.

(*Sound of door opening, voices become fainter as they move into hallway*)

MOORHEAD: I just thought it was ... absolutely amazing.
SOKOLOV: Mmm.
MOORHEAD: I mean, it really blew my mind.

(*Poof! And she's gone!*)
(*Scene*)

"Something funny, Oliver?"

At this moment, I realize I'm laughing out loud.

Moorhead glares at me from the dry-erase board. "Sorry if I seem surprised. I'm just not used to students laughing while I describe an all too plausible dystopian future, where books are illegal and people who think freely are *penalized* for—"

I laugh again, even louder, and clap my hands. His glare hardens into something glassy. Pammy Quattlebaum purses her lips and shakes her moonlike head at me.

I smile feebly: "You said *penal*."

The entire class explodes into joyful, sub-human glee. Moorhead sighs and turns his back on me; I am a lost cause.

The real lost cause, of course, is his attempt to woo *La Sokolova*. The lady is out of his league. She's ten times smarter than he is, and much better looking, even if she is too skinny. She's the kind of woman his sort can only press its nose against the glass and watch as they walk past. I guess he thinks he has a chance because she's trapped in the same school with him.

The irony is that Moorhead is definitely much happier *without* her than he ever would be *with* her. Despite her beauty and intelligence, Sokolov is a short-tempered, hypercritical witch. She may be the meanest woman I've ever met. She once told Benito Guzman, the Shyest Boy in School, that he had the personality of a used diaper. If Moorhead were ever unlucky enough to actually be in a relationship with her ... well, a woman like that would just *crush* him.

Hmmm.

There might be something to work with here.

I stick around after class. I want to see Moorhead read his latest cigarette: YOU NEED TO TRY A NEW DEODORANT.

Social studies might be my least favorite class—which is strange, because I kind of like the teacher. It's just so dull. I feel like we're all being taught how boring the people in other countries are.

I raise my hand. My social studies teacher, Mrs. Magoffin, says, "What is it, Oliver?"

"My stomach hurts."

Tatiana says, "That's serious, Miz Magoffin. When his stomach hurts, they can feel it in China."

Mrs. Magoffin ignores Tatiana. "Well, Oliver, I'm not surprised. I saw you eating beef jerky and chunky peanut butter in the hallway before class. But if it'll make you feel any better, you may go to the restroom."

Mrs. Magoffin is normally a painfully polite woman, so I'm surprised she's called attention to my mid-afternoon snack.[40] But I thank her and head to the boys' room.

It's empty, as I expected. I head for the third stall, which

---

40. I work up a real appetite in P.E.

has a permanent OUT OF ORDER sign on its door. Even if you wanted to ignore the sign, you couldn't; the door is sealed shut by electromagnets and won't open unless you jiggle the handle in the proper combination.[41]

Inside, the porcelain looks as stained and crusted and cruddy as any other toilet at school, but that's all just paint and makeup. This toilet isn't really a toilet, and I insist that it be kept scrupulously clean.

I lift the lid off the "water tank" behind the "toilet"—it's full of Milk Duds, fresh popcorn, and soda pop. I grab a bag of popcorn, then I "flush" the toilet. The light fixture overhead starts projecting a movie onto the water in the bowl.

The film was taken about twenty minutes after I saw Mr. Pinckney this morning. The setting is his office. He's at his desk, doing paperwork and grumbling about it. Then The Motivator walks in.

I pop in my earbud and click it over to the movie channel so I can listen.

Mr. Pinckney says, "Who are you?"

The Motivator smiles (and it is a terrifying smile) and says, "I suggest you reconsider putting Oliver Watson on the ballot for class president."

---

41. Why are you looking down here? Did you honestly think I would give you the combination? My God, you're stupider than you look.

Pinckney looks at him funny. "Who are you? Oliver's father?"

The Motivator just broadens his smile. "I suggest you reconsider putting Oliver Watson on the ballot for class president."

"Look, whoever you are, you can't just barge in here making demands. Don't make me call security." Pinckney picks up his phone. The line is dead, of course.

Now The Motivator's smile reaches from ear to pointed ear. "I suggest you reconsider putting Oliver Watson on the ballot for class president."

Most people cave in at this point. They just get too spooked. They look at this man—this *monster*—standing in front of them, this seven foot tall, bald-headed, black-clad *beast*, and they say, "Yes, yes! Whatever you want! Just leave!"

But Pinckney's a tough man. "I don't know who you are," he says. "Quite frankly, I don't know *what* you are. But you have no right to tell me how to run my school. My decision on the Watson boy is final."

I put my popcorn under the toilet paper dispenser and press down on it. Hot butter squirts out. This is getting exciting!

The Motivator laces his massive fingers together. His hands look like bleached-white baseball mitts, covered with hairy moles and warts. He can see that Phase One isn't working on Pinckney, so he moves to Phase Three[42]—bribery.

"I will give you anything—and I mean *anything* in the world—if you reconsider putting Oliver Watson on the ballot for class president."

Now Pinckney smiles, incredulous. "Are you serious? You're actually trying to *bribe* me? For a student-council election?"

The Motivator doesn't move. He doesn't appear to breathe. He just smiles, smiles, smiles. His big square teeth jut out of his skull like two rows of broken yellow tombstones.

Pinckney laughs. "Okay, fine. Anything? All right then: I want a Rocket-Firing Boba Fett action figure. You get me that, and I'll do whatever you want. Sky's the limit."

The Motivator stops smiling. He nods and exits.

Pinckney stares at the empty doorway, still not sure he didn't hallucinate the whole thing. Then the phone receiver, which he's still holding, starts buzzing with a dial tone. The movie flickers to a stop.

This is going to be a little more difficult than I'd hoped.

---

42. Phase Two wouldn't work in this case. Pinckney's the type who calls the cops when you try to blackmail him.

I've run up against this Boba Fett doll before. In 1979, the company that made *Star Wars* toys made a special offer to fans: Send in four proofs of purchase and get a free dolly of Boba Fett the bounty hunter that fires *actual rockets* out of its backpack (*see plate 8*). Yes, real, actual, cheap crummy plastic "rockets" that flew about six inches when you released the cheap crummy spring they were loaded into.

Naturally, the children of the world went nuts with excitement for this thing. Because the children of the world are *brilliant*.

PLATE 8: Send in four proofs of purchase, and get a free dolly of Boba Fett the bounty hunter that fires actual rockets out of its backpack.

Unfortunately, after a few prototypes were made, the company realized that all those brilliant children would choke to death trying to swallow the plastic rockets.

So the Rocket-Firing Boba Fett doll was never released. This led to considerable disappointment. In fact, for science geeks of a certain age, this doll represents the Holy Grail of *Star Wars* memorabilia. It is the toy they've always wanted—the toy they were *promised*—but never got. This is the toy that will make their lives complete.

Only two dozen prototypes were made. Less than half of those survive. Only one is finished enough—painted, with working spring and original rocket—to count as an actual Rocket-Firing Boba Fett Doll.

It's owned by the dictator of a certain African nation, who, I happen to know, won't sell it for any price.[43] Which says something, because otherwise he'll do anything for money.

I sit on the toilet and munch Milk Duds until the bell rings. I have some more heavy thinking to do. I'll tell Sheldrake to gas up the blimp.

---

43. I was going to melt it down and send the remains to Bill Gates. I'm a real jerk sometimes.

Chapter 10:
BOYS ARE IDIOTS

Girls are idiots, too, of course, but boys are a special kind of idiot.

A girl, for instance, will vote for a boy in an election, or go to a movie that's about a boy, or buy a book that features a boy hero.[44] Boys are much less likely to return the favor. They can't wrap their feeble minds around the idea that this *girl* might have anything in common with them. It's like they can't recognize girls as human beings.

Which puts Liz Twombley at a distinct disadvantage in this election, even though she is the Most Popular Girl in School.

Liz is a sweet dimwit with mediocre good looks and a friendly smile. She's much nicer than most Most Popular Girls in School tend to be, so she probably won't last long. She owes her status to the fact that 1) she's rich—her father is the world's leading manufacturer of those

---

44. Or villain.

giant blow-up gorillas you see on top of car dealerships (*see plate 9*), and 2) she developed early. That is to say, she's got boobs.

Now, developing early can be a double-edged (though strangely soft and pillowy) sword. Girls who develop early are either the Most Popular Girl in School or sluts. That is to say, they're not *really* sluts. Everyone just calls them sluts because they have boobs. This is what passes for logic among my peers.[45]

Liz has escaped the unfair labeling by growing boobs *without noticing she's got them*. Completely free of self-consciousness, she plows through the world oblivious to the twin heralds that announce her presence. You can't call someone a slut when they're clearly so naive. It's a tricky move that requires a dangerous level of stupidity to pull off. Generally, late puberty is a much less risky play. Though, in my own personal case, I am thoroughly sick of it.

"Representing Mr. Moorhead's homeroom, Elizabeth Twombley."

Liz bobs to the front of the auditorium, artlessly slapping her flat feet down the aisle like a scuba diver in a beauty contest. Once onstage, it's hard to tell what's bigger, her smile or her— Actually, I regret starting that sentence. The point is, she's there, and the crowd gives up a tepid round of applause.

---

45. Daddy calls them "the future." Chilling thought.

PLATE 9: She's rich—her father is the world's leading manufacturer of those giant blow-up gorillas you see on top of car dealerships.

Liz's friends jump up in their seats and start chanting, "Go Twombley! You're the bomb-ley! Go Twombley! Go Twombley!" A few of the Not Quite Popular Girls jump up and join in, peeking out of the corners of their eyes to see if the Popular Girls notice (they don't).

Everyone else is busy whispering, poking, giggling, napping. I'm seated near the back, middle of the row, and feeling very crowded. Normally, there would be empty seats around me, but today the auditorium is packed; the entire school is at this assembly. Every red-velvet seat is filled. Some people are sitting Indian style in the aisles. I am sitting between the Chinese Exchange Student, who's snoring,[46] and Randy Sparks, the Most Pathetic Boy in School, who's trying to smell his breath by blowing into his hand.

Up onstage, Liz stands in front of the nominees for the lesser eighth-grade class offices—a collection of lurkers, butt-scratchers, and rats taking their first steps toward a glorious future as low-level bureaucrats.[47]

Next to Liz stands Vice Principal Hruska, a grizzled old pro one year shy of retirement, who's stuck with the job of announcing the student council nominees. He consults

46. And sporting the most lavish growth of nostril hair I've ever seen on a seventh grader.

47. BUREAUCRAT (*n.*): Someone who sits behind a desk and tells you that you can't do something.

the printout in his hand. "From Ms. Sokolov's homeroom, Jack Chapman."

Jack moves gracefully down the aisle to thunderous applause. Liz's friends make sour faces and sit down, but they're replaced by a hundred children who jump to their feet and cheer lustily. You'd think he was running for king. He and Liz exchange friendly smiles.

Old man Hruska looks at Jack and Liz, but it's like he doesn't see them. He's got the hundred-yard stare common to long-term prison inmates or teachers who are close to getting their pensions. You're not going to catch him getting misty-eyed over another stupid student-council election. He's like a statue who's given up caring if the birds poop on it or not—a statue with a perfectly brushed blue-gray crew cut and two dozen gravy stains on its tie. He just wants to wrap this farce up. He glances down at the speech, ready to see the words "Thank you all for coming, please return to class in an orderly fashion" when he sees something unexpected. His face falls. He looks confused and suddenly very, very tired.

I feel sorry for him. This is really supposed to be Principal Pinckney's job—that's Pinckney's speech he's reading. But Pinckney canceled at the last minute, handed the speech to Hruska, then closed and locked his office door. He's spent the last three hours in there, playing with a thirty-year-old toy The Motivator hand-delivered to him this morning.

A Rocket-Firing Boba Fett doll.

Hruska coughs out the next sentence: "Also from Ms. Sokolov's class ... Oli ... Oliver Watson."

The room stops breathing. Randy Sparks chokes on the fingernail he's chewing. I make my face a perfect blank, mumble a few polite 'scuse mes as I slide past people's legs, and walk halfway down the aisle in complete silence.

Perfect, perfect silence.

And then the whole world is shattered by a wave of primitive *shouting*, laughing, *screaming*, giggling, *yelling*, clapping, *stomping*. My classmates have never seen anything so delightful. The room shakes with their glee.

Tatiana, who is the queen of mixed messages, smiles warmly and gives me an insulting hand gesture as I pass.

As I mount the stage, Liz and Jack stare at me with confusion. Hruska stares at me with concern. "Oliver," he whispers, "what's going on?"

"I want to be class president."

He shrugs his eyebrows with a look that says, "No one better try to blame this on me." Then he turns back to the microphone: "Your attention, please. Your attention, please. If everyone could please settle down ..."

The animal sounds from the audience don't get any softer. "Your attention, please. Your attention, please ..."

More hooting. More yelling. More laughing. The sound vibrations are so intense, it's hard to see straight—like looking through the air above a barbecue grill.

"Attention. Attention. Your attention, plea—"

A scream from the front row: "What's he gonna do? *Eat* the other candidates?"

That does it for the old man. He balls up the speech, throws it at a freckled girl who's running for class treasurer (and cackling like a hyena), and bellows with both his wrinkled old lungs: "All right, you creeps! Just shut up and go back to class already!"

It takes half an hour for the auditorium to clear.

Later that afternoon, in Mrs. Magoffin's social studies class, we sit with our desks in a circle and discuss the big news story of the day: An evil African dictator has been over-thrown by a democratic insurgency. The dictator barely escaped with his life and had to leave many of his most prized possessions—and toys—behind.

Jordie Moscowitz raises his hand and whines, "What does all this Africa stuff have to do with us?"

In Jordie's case, not a lot. Personally, it means I'm now only the fourth-richest person on earth. Revolutions don't come cheap.

Chapter 11:
A BRIEF DISCOURSE ON EVIL

"What is evil?" you ask.

To which I reply, "Who are you? Friedrich Nietzsche?"

To which you respond, "Duh ... wha? Me no understand."

Then I put you back in your cage.

I freely admit I'm evil. At least, I freely admit it when I'm alone and no one can hear me. That doesn't mean I torture kittens or plot the genocide of entire continents of people; that's insanity, not evil. And insanity is just what we call stupidity when it doesn't make sense.

I am evil because I really don't care about what's best for the world. I care about what's best for me. I have no particular respect for this earth or the two-legged vermin who infest it.

I suspect more people are evil than they'd admit. There's just nothing they can do about it.

Lucky for me, I'm a genius, and I can pretty much do whatever I want. And what I want—and this is what makes me *super* evil—is to *enforce my will on the inhabitants of this planet.* I want power, control. I want things to go exactly how I want, when I want, for as long as I want.[48]

This puts me in good company: Napoleon, Augustus Caesar. It also puts me in with some real stinkers: Idi Amin, Stalin. But again, those last two don't really deserve the honor of being called evil—they're just bug-eyed, spittle-spewing, ape-turd insane.

It's why we call one dictator Alexander the Great, and another Hitler, the little creep with the moustache.

The fact is, when I ascend to my throne—and I *will* ascend to my throne—life for the average person won't be much worse than it is now. In some respects, it will probably be better. For instance, I will outlaw the song "Jingle Bell Rock," which all scientists agree is the worst song ever created.[49] With that one law, I will improve Christmas by two hundred percent!

"But what's the point of being evil?" you ask. "Why can't you just live and let live?"

---

48. Basically, I want to be two years old forever.

49. The punishment for anyone caught playing it would involve being forced to listen to "Jingle Bell Rock" over and over again.

In answer, I point to my beloved Captain Beefheart, a musician so brilliant, so evil, *he drove his own band insane.*[50] He would not let them eat. He would not let them sleep. He would not  let them leave his house. He made them wear dresses (and they were not girls). He stripped them of their very names and subjected them to hours and hours of abusive group-therapy sessions. When a dejected and desperate member of the Magic Band managed to escape the Captain's clutches, Beefheart snatched him off the street and *dragged him back* to the practice studio.

It was cruel. Assuredly. Inhumane. Undoubtedly. Evil. Disgustingly so. And yet I defy you, today, to listen to *Trout Mask Replica* and say it was not worth it.[51]

But enough discourse. Let's return to the evil at hand.

---

50. Allegedly. I wasn't there—I've just read a few magazine articles, which could be complete lies. But it would be a shame if it weren't true.

51. Actually, *you* probably *would* say it wasn't worth it. Back in the cage!

Down in my Control Center, Sheldrake and I sit in vibrating leather massage chairs as we read Research's probes into Jack Chapman and Liz Twombley. The air around us is full of sporadic *zapping* noises; on the catwalk above us, my technicians are testing my latest invention—the Electrolyzer. It's a wand I can point at anything to give it an electric charge. To put it in terms your small brain can understand: You know how sometimes when you touch a doorknob, it stings your widdle fingers? With the Electrolyzer, I can turn any doorknob in the world into one that stings, as long as I can see it. The power transfer is inefficient, but I think it will have its uses.

Liz's file is a little thin. Jack's file, on the other hand, is equally thin, but massively satisfying. It'll do nicely.

"Research," I announce, "you are all permitted to go to the movies tonight. My treat."

From somewhere in the bowels of my lair, I hear a dozen voices make a distant "hurrah." No one can accuse me of being stingy.

"We're done. It works."

I look up. One of my newest technicians, a cross-eyed wild-haired young brat (is his name Chauncey?) leans over the edge of the catwalk, supporting himself with one hand on the metal lattice work. His other hand holds "it"—the Electrolyzer.

"So soon?" I ask. "Have you gone through the testing protocol a thousand times already?"

Chauncey sniggers. He wears his lab coat unbuttoned, exposing a Jonas Brothers T-shirt.[52] "No offense, boss man, but I graduated top of my class at M.I.T." I notice that the other technicians, the ones who've worked for me longer, are standing as far away from him as possible. "I don't need to test something a thousand times to know it works. It works."

"Really?" I say. "Let me see." I motion for him to drop the Electrolyzer to me. He tosses it, carefully, and Lolli leaps into the air like a black-and-tan rainbow and catches it in her pearly whites. She drops the foot-long rubber-and-steel wand into my lap. I examine it closely, then turn it on. It starts to hum, and my nostrils are instantly filled with the burned-aluminum smell of ozone.

"See?" says Chauncey. "It's in perfect conditi—"

I point it at the girder he's holding onto and squeeze the trigger. "Ow!" squawks Chauncey, who lets go of the now-electrified girder and falls fifteen feet to the floor.

---

52. Ugh. He's probably wearing it ironically, but still: ugh.

"You're right," I say. "It works."

Chauncey grimaces and tests his ankle, which he seems to have sprained somehow.

An amplified knocking sound resounds through the cavern. Daddy's voice rings out over the loudspeakers.

"Oliver, get out here and come to the table. Your dinner's getting cold."

"I'll be right there, Daddy," I sing sweetly. My intercom is tuned to make it sound like I'm in my bedroom, just a few inches of plywood away from him.

"That's what you said ten minutes ago. Don't make me knock down this door."[53]

Sheldrake turns aside and coughs into his fist. He's embarrassed for me. My other underlings become conspicuously more interested in their work, as if they hadn't heard a word of the preceding conversation. They all know that if I catch them giggling— or even smirking—at my plight, they'll wake up tomorrow stuffed into a bag of crocodile chow at the Saint Louis Zoo.

My father has shamed me in front of my minions. Again.

---

53. I'd like to see him try. An Abrams tank couldn't knock down that door.

And I'd like to say this is the last time. But as Lollipop and I sprint for the elevator (and I can positively feel Chauncey smirking behind me), I know it will happen again and again and again, until that glorious day six years from now when I can claim my kingdom.

Tonight, at any rate, I'll get my first taste of revenge. I sit across from Daddy at the table, watching him mince his food in his thin-lipped mouth, waiting for the right moment to drop my bomb.

"Who are you supposed to be," asks Daddy, "the Purple Phantom?"

This makes less sense than most things he says—which is saying a lot. He reaches out with his fork and taps me on the shoulder. I realize I am still wearing my cape.

"Costume," I mumble. "For the school play."

Mom nearly drops the macaroni casserole. "Are you in the school play, Sugarplum?"

"No," I say. "They gave me the cape so I wouldn't bother them when they rehearsed."

"Wasn't that nice!" says Mom. She strokes the cape appreciatively. "Mmmm. Is that silk?"

"Don't be silly, Marlene. Who would give him a silk cape?" says Daddy, making a snorting sound I don't care for very much. I click my heels twice. Lollipop leaps into his lap like a kitten and rubs her rough rubber tongue across his neck. Her pretty teeth tickle his windpipe, carotid artery, and jugular vein.

Daddy isn't snorting anymore. "Oliver! Control your dog!" he screams, holding up his plate with both hands like a shield (and spilling macaroni all over the floor).

"Lolli loves you, Daddy," I say, but I click my heels one more time. She drops from his lap and starts scarfing up his lost pasta.

Mom passes the casserole to Daddy so he can refill his plate. "They had an assembly at Oliver's school today to announce who's running for student council."

"Oh?" says Daddy, as he selects the three smallest macaronis from the platter and passes it to me. "Who ended up running for president?"

"Liz Twombley. Jack Chapman ..." I say, as I erect a Mount McKinley of macaroni on my plate. "And me."

"No, not you," says Daddy, with a mean eye on my mac. "Remember? You declined the nomination."

"I changed my mind. Mr. Pinckney put me on the ballot. Now I'm running for president."

"You never told me that!" screams Mom, who is driven to her feet by the force of this momentous news. "You never told me!" She rushes around the table to hug and kiss me something delightfully awful. I will be sore tomorrow.

Daddy spits the macaroni he's sucking on into his napkin. "That's . . . terrific, son."

"I'm gonna be somebody 'portant. Just like you, Daddy!"

"Erm . . . yes. Well, try not to count your chickens too fast. It's a long road from nomination to election day."

"*Of course, he'll win*!" shrieks Mom, who emphasizes this statement of confidence by biting my right ear. "*Of course, he will*! Who could vote against Oliver? Who would *dare*?!"

My father takes a long drink of water. "Erm . . . of course. Obviously we would vote for him, dear," he says, looking none too sure about that. "I just don't want Ollie to be disappointed if he doesn't—Marlene, the boy needs to breathe."

Mom relaxes her hold on my neck, barely. I suck in some much-needed O_2. Just in time too—another few seconds and one of my bodyguards would have burst through the window to remove her. And that would have been hard to explain.

After some coaxing, Mom is convinced to return to her seat. She sits there now, tears streaming down her jiggling cheeks as she stuffs macaroni into her smiling maw.

Daddy gives me a reassuring tap on the hand. "Son, what you're doing is very brave. Probably braver than you even know. So, uh ... good ... erm ... luck."

I fix him with a demonic smile. "I'm gonna be just like you, Daddy. Just like *you*."

My father turns his head aside and coughs into his fist.

"Mmb mmbm mmmbbm," says Mom, through her mouth full of gluey pasta. It takes a son's ears to decipher her words:

"Of course, he will."

Chapter 12:

A PHONE CALL TO THE LUXURIA CORPORATION[54] CUSTOMER SERVICE HELP LINE.

(*Ringing, then a click*)

OPERATOR: Customer service. This call may be monitored. How may I assist you?

MAN: Hi. Uh...I have a...Are you guys...

(*Awkward silence*)

OPERATOR: Are you still there, sir?

MAN: Yeah. It's just that...I have kind of a strange question.

OPERATOR: There are no strange questions when it comes to customer satisfaction.

MAN: Yeah. Okay. Well, the thing is...are you guys putting messages on the cigarettes?

OPERATOR: Messages?

MAN: I mean, not on every cigarette. Just on some of them.

OPERATOR: If you're referring to the Surgeon General's Warning, that's on the outside of the—

MAN: No, it's not that. These are messages printed on the cigarettes.

OPERATOR: Printed?

---

54. Formerly known as the "J.H. Bruce Tobacco Company."

MAN: Typed.

OPERATOR: How would you type on a cigarette?

MAN: I don't know.

OPERATOR: What sort of messages are they, sir?

MAN: Kind of like mean fortune cookies. About, uh ... maybe changing your deodorant. Or starting a new diet.

OPERATOR: Uh-huh.

MAN: I got one today. It says, "IT'S PRONOUNCED NA-*BO*-KOV."[55]

OPERATOR: It says what?

MAN: He was a writer. It tells you how to say his name. Look, I still have it. I can send it to you.

OPERATOR: Why would you do that?

MAN: To show you it's typed on!

OPERATOR: I'm confused. Are you trying to sell us a typewriter that types on cigarettes? If so, you should contact business affairs. Their hours are—

MAN: You really don't know what I'm talking about.

OPERATOR: I'm afraid not.

(*Sound of man cursing under his breath*)

OPERATOR: Um, sir, forgive me for asking, but are you on any sort of medication that might be altering your perception of reality—

MAN: I'm not on any medication!

OPERATOR. I see. So you're off your medication. Is there a doctor or family member you can contact—

(*End of call*)

---

55. Basic Russian pronunciation. Emphasis goes on the second-to-last syllable.

Chapter 13:
THWARTED

Something strange is going on with my classmates. They've been giving me weird looks all morning. Not mean looks, just *weird*. Any looks are weird, of course, since normally they don't notice me at all. But these looks are *especially* weird. Sad, almost. And they're whispering to each other even more than usual.

I didn't pay much attention to this at first. After all, if you're the only human at the zoo, you don't really care when the monkeys start throwing poo at each other.

But I have just bumped into Liz Twombley in the hallway (normally a pleasant experience) and, to my amazement, I see *real tears* welling up in her china blue eyes.

"Did I hurtcha, Liz?" I mumble.

"Oh, Oliver!" she gasps, all heaves and suppressed emotion. She throws a hand over those previously mentioned china blues and rushes into the ladies room.

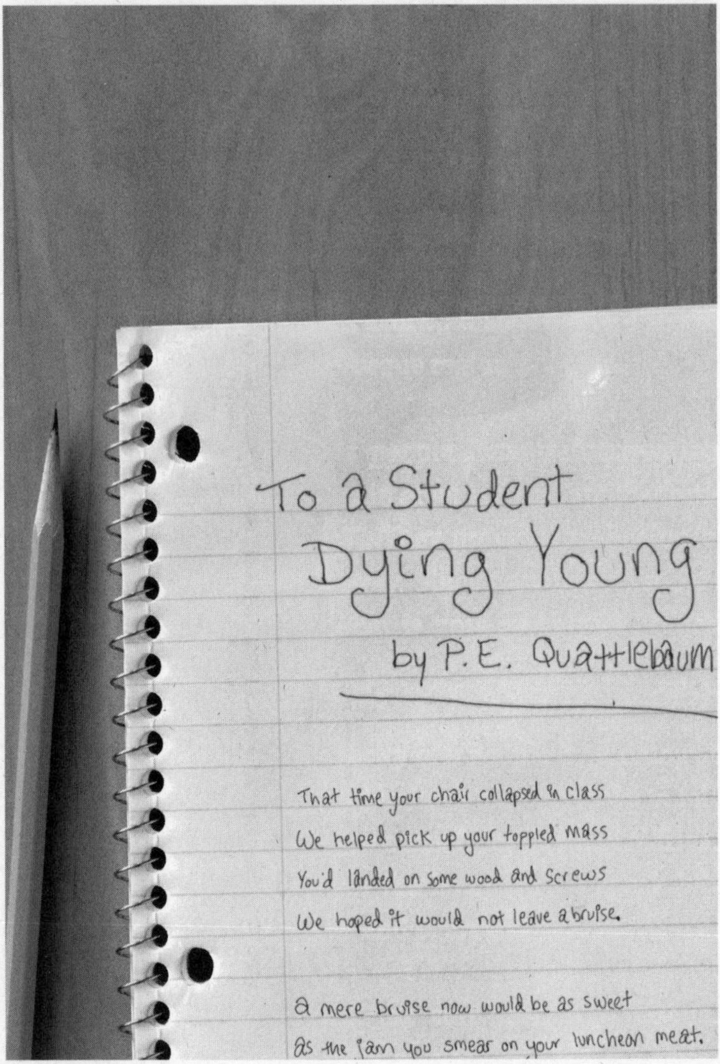

PLATE 10: Pammy Quattlebaum has left a poem on my seat.

Something is *definitely* going on.

I step cautiously into English class. The room is a beehive of buzzing whispers that silences the second I walk in. Everyone is staring at me, but they all look away as soon as I look back at them. All except for Tatiana. She lowers her expensive pink sunglasses[56] and gives me a long slow wink, then resumes writing VOTE 4 TUBBY on the wall with a felt-tip marker.

The mystery deepens when I reach my desk and see that Pammy Quattlebaum has left a poem on my seat (*see plate 10*).

TO A STUDENT DYING YOUNG

By P.E. Quattlebaum

That time your chair collapsed in class
We helped pick up your toppled mass
You'd landed on some wood and screws
We hoped it would not leave a bruise.

A mere bruise now would be as sweet
As the jam you smear on your luncheon meat—

There's more, much more, but that's all I can stand to read right now. I look up at her with annoyance and confusion

---

56. She won them when her mother was the millionth customer at a local bank.

(and, I'm afraid, some intelligence) plainly on my face, only to find her looking right back at me. Her ridiculous cow eyes are full to the brim with sympathy.

I scan the room. *Everyone's* ridiculous eyes are full to the brim with sympathy. Only Tatiana seems normal (for her). She clutches her scrawny belly gleefully, like it's about to crack open with laughter.

Moorhead enters, but he doesn't leave the doorway. "Pammy, can you lead everyone in a discussion of the symbolic meaning of television in *Fahrenheit 451*?"

"Of course, Mr. Moorhead."

Moorhead turns a sickly yellow-toothed smile in my direction. "Oliver, I'd like to see you in the hallway for a minute."

All eyes are on me as I follow him out. Moorhead closes the door behind us, and we are alone in the deserted hallway. This close to him, I notice he doesn't smell quite as noxious as usual. He's taken my advice about the deodorant.

"Oliver, I have to say, I was as surprised as anyone when you decided to run for president."

I look back at him with genuine puzzlement.

"But now . . . well . . . in light of what we've all heard . . . and you should know, your secret is out . . . well, it makes a lot more sense."

To him, maybe.

"Just know that we're all rooting for you. And not just in the election. Every day you hear about another medical miracle, some new treatment. . . ."

And suddenly the answer washes over me like a tidal wave of rainbow sherbet.

They think I'm dying.

"They have wonder drugs these days that were *unthinkable* when I was your—"

These idiots think I'm dying! And they think I'm running for president as some sort of last-ditch make-a-wish plan to get the most out of life. It all makes sense now—it's the only way their puny brains could fathom my decision to run.[57]

"But you've got to stay upbeat. Optimistic. That's the most important thing you can do."

---

57. Although this does make Tati's attitude seem a little more callous than usual. Tomorrow the bank will call her mother, say she was actually only the 999,999th customer, and demand those sunglasses back.

I display my teeth like two lines of sticky pearls. "My Daddy says I'm very brave."

"I'm sure he does," says Moorhead as he rests his comforting caterpillars on my shoulder.

Randy Sparks, the Most Pathetic Boy in School, approaches with a slip of paper in his hand. "Mr. Pinckney wants to see Oliver in his office." Randy turns to me. "I'm really sorry, Oliver."

"Stop shouting at me, Randy!" I clap my hands over my ears.

Randy steps back, scared. Moorhead whispers to him, "He's very sensitive right now." Then Moorhead slaps me on the back. "You better go see what Mr. Pinckney wants."

"Yes, Mr. Moorhead."

He gives me a thumbs-up as I walk away. "Live strong, dude."

Even Randy almost laughs at that one.

I walk to Pinckney's office on a cloud of delight. The rash-red floors have never looked warmer, the puke-green lockers have never looked more vibrant and puke-ish. I've as good as won the election, and it's still almost a month away. "O frabjous day!" Every child in my class will vote for me out of misguided sympathy. So simple, so elegant—I couldn't have thought of anything better myself. It just proves what I've always said: You don't have to be a genius when you're surrounded by morons.

Every school chum I see only adds to my glee. There's Jordie Moscowitz, looking sorry he ever teased me. And there's Alan Pitt—my, aren't his zits huge today! His face looks like a can of tomato sauce threw up on it![58]

And then I get to Pinckney's door. And I hear something that sends my wave of rainbow-sherbet joy crashing on the fungus-crusted rocks of hard reality.

I push it open slowly, reluctantly. All my worst fears are confirmed. Mom sits there, looking even more melted and shapeless than usual. She weeps copiously as my father (rather unenthusiastically) tries to comfort her. "Oliver's dying!" she moans. "Dying!"

"No, he isn't, Marlene. Now calm yourself—"

Mom points a finger at Pinckney. "But he said—" Then she sees me. "Oliver!"

---

58. Maybe that will teach him not to yell out unkind remarks about certain candidates eating certain other candidates during school assemblies. His dermatologist is one of my agents.

The next five minutes are a blur of hugging and tugging and kissing and crying.

After every Kleenex in the room has been filled with snot, Pinckney brings the meeting to some semblance of order. "Naturally, I was suspicious of the rumor from the start. I had never heard of a disease called progressive"—he checks his notes—"lardonoma. But I needed to make sure. And since you assure me Oliver isn't sick..."

Daddy scowls. "Not in the slightest. He just got a physical last month, and aside from the obvious weight issue—"

"Oliver's dying!"

My father has reached his limit. "For Pete's sake, Marlene! We're *all* dying!"

She's not in the mood for a philosophy lesson. As the two of them devolve into a confusion of tears and sniping and apologies, Pinckney takes me aside. "There will be announcements in every homeroom tomorrow, letting everyone know the good news about your health. There's no reason this should interfere with your candidacy...."

Daddy overhears this. "Oh yeah—thanks for putting him on the ballot." His argument with Mom has put him on edge. "That was a *great* decision, Principal. He won't embarrass himself *at all*."

"You're welcome," says Pinckney, opting to ignore the sarcasm. He gives a quick worried glance at a locked filing cabinet behind him.

After a final round of sloppy smooches, I'm sent on my way. That leering, lying red hall, so recently alive with promise, now seems dull and lifeless. This world is empty, treacherous, and small.

Victory had hopped into my hands, like a baby bird.

And then Daddy came along and stomped the pretty thing. Mom would never have given me away, but oh, that Daddy...

"Beefheart," I command, in the depth of my despair. There are ten seconds of silence, a sudden *click*... and then, in an incident no school electrician will ever be able to explain, the atonal wonders of my new favorite song, "The Blimp," start blasting over the public-address system.

The lockers on both sides of the hall shudder rhythmically as I walk past them on my way back to class. My day will come.

Chapter 14:

OLIVER WATSON'S THEATER OF THE MIND PRESENTS THREE PLAYS FOR YOUR AMUSEMENT[59]

PICK A WINNER!

(*Setting: a public basketball court. Time: early evening*)

(*Sound of applause, hand-slapping, boys saying goodbye*)

OPERATIVE 919: Hey, kid. Nice game.

JACK CHAPMAN: Thanks.

OP 919: You're Jack, right? Jack Chapman?

JACK: I don't know you.

OP 919: What's the matter? You're not supposed to talk to strange men? Well, I'm a strange woman, so relax....

JACK: Goodbye.

OP 919: I just thought you might like to see these pictures I got.

JACK: I'm not interested in any—

(*Sound of papers being pulled out of envelope*)

JACK: Oh my God.

OP 919: Here. Take a good long look.

(*Sound of papers being frantically shuffled*)

---

59. All transcripts copied verbatim from the original recordings. All of my agents wear recording devices.

JACK: Oh.

OP 919: That's you, right? Picking your nose, eating your boogers?

JACK: Oh.

OP 919: Sucking the scum out from under your fingernails?

JACK: Oh ...

OP 919: It's not for me to say, or anything, but you're a little old for that, aren't you?

JACK: How did you—?

OP 919: Besides the obvious health risk. You could give yourself a cold or something. Didja ever think about that?

JACK: How did you get these?

OP 919: Funny story. I live in Turkey. Yesterday a guy calls me, tells me to get on a plane to Omaha. Had to make like five connections. So when I land, another guy hands me this envelope, along with your name, this address, and a message.

JACK: Message? ...

OP 919: "Drop out of the student-council election."

JACK: Why would anyone? ...

OP 919: No idea. Damnedest thing I ever heard of. Anyway, now that we're done, I'm heading back to the airport, catching the first flight home.

JACK: Wait! Will anyone? ...

GIRL'S VOICE (*in distance*): Great game, Jack!

(*Sound of frantic envelope stuffing*)

JACK (*false hearty*): Thanks, Shirelle! (*then, quieter*) Will anyone see these?

OP 919: Not if you drop out of the election.

JACK: Okay. Fine. I'll do it. I'll do it!

OP 919: Try to see the upside. Now you got a reason to break a really nasty habit. So, maybe in the long run, we're doing you a favor.

JACK (*sighs*): Right.

OP 919: It's been a pleasure doing business. Forgive me if I don't shake hands.

(*Sound of stiletto heels walking away*)

(*Fin*)

THE KID STAYS IN THE PICTURE

(*Setting: teachers' lounge. Time: mid-morning*)

(*Sound of teachers lounging*)

MOORHEAD: Hi, Lucy.

SOKOLOV: Mmm.

MOORHEAD: Still reading (*pronounces it correctly*) Nabokov, huh?

(*Sound of book being reluctantly put down*)

SOKOLOV: I'm trying to.

MOORHEAD: That's awesome. Coffee?

SOKOLOV: I don't drink coffee.

MOORHEAD: Thought you might have changed your

mind. Personally, I drink way too much (*lame giggle*).

SOKOLOV: Gee. How awful for you.[60]

MOORHEAD: Well … enjoy your (*pronounces it correctly*) Nabokov.

SOKOLOV: I will!

(*Sound of leather man-sandals walking away*)

SOKOLOV (*under her breath*): Twit.[61]

(*Fin*)

DANCIN' FOOL

(*Setting: a suburban kitchen. Time: late afternoon*)

(*Sound of someone licking the crème filling from Oreos, a window opening*)

LIZ TWOMBLEY: Wow! Did you just come through the window?

THE MOTIVATOR:[62] No room is closed to me.

LIZ: You're funny looking.

---

60. I was drinking strawberry-flavored milk when I listened to this. I laughed so hard, the milk went out my nose—not unusual. But *then* my oxygen-deprived lungs sucked in air so hard *I sucked the milk back into my mouth and it went out my nose again*! Playing with Moorhead and Sokolov is even more fun than I'd planned!

61. Progress. Previously she would have called him "imbecile."

62. The blackmail material for Liz is weaker than the Jack stuff, so I've sent The Motivator, my most trusted agent, to seal the deal. He persuades through fear. No human being can look upon his horrible face without quaking in terror.

MOTIVATOR: Erm ...

LIZ: I'm sorry, that was rude. You're not funny looking at all. I hardly noticed.

MOTIVATOR: I suggest you drop out of the election for class president.

LIZ: That's so weird! I already almost *did* drop out, because there's this boy who has this disease of fatness that's killing him, but it turns out it wasn't true.

MOTIVATOR: I suggest you drop out—

LIZ: But I don't see how it's not true, because he's still totally fat.

MOTIVATOR: (*coughs*) Erm ... Really? I don't think he's fat.

LIZ: Are you crazy? He's huge!

MOTIVATOR: Erm ... no ... I hear he looks powerful. Handsome.

LIZ: Huh. I guess he's kind of cute. Like one of those poison fish that blow up, if you could pet them. Do you want the cookie part of my Oreos? I only eat the stuf.

MOTIVATOR: I suggest you drop out of the election for class president.

(*Sound of papers being taken out of an envelope*)

LIZ: Oh my God! That's me!

MOTIVATOR: I suggest—

LIZ: (*delighted laughter*) Dancing around in my jammies, singing into my hairbrush. I remember doing that! That is so embarrassing!

MOTIVATOR: Yes, exactly. So, I sug—

LIZ: You know what? If my friends saw these? How embarrassing would that be! Where did you get them? Can I get more?

MOTIVATOR: We can make an unlimited supply of—

LIZ: Oh my God! What if we blew them up, like, poster-size, and put them up all over school. That would be so embarrassing! (*Ten-second-long giggle fit*).

MOTIVATOR: (*long pause*) Do you know what the word embarrassing means?

LIZ: It means hilarious! Can I have these pictures?

MOTIVATOR: Knock yourself out.

LIZ: I'm going to be totally humiliated!

MOTIVATOR: What if I was to offer you anything in the world if you agreed to drop out of the election?[63]

LIZ: Anything?

MOTIVATOR: Anything.

LIZ: World Peace.

MOTIVATOR: You can't have that.

LIZ: You said anything!

MOTIVATOR: Besides that.

LIZ: Mmm ... a pet unicorn.

MOTIVATOR (*urgently*): Permission to go to Phase Four! Please, give me permission to go to Phase Four!

LIZ: Who are you talking to?

(*A beat of silence*)[64]

MOTIVATOR: Damn it.

(*A beat of silence*)

---

63. Note the shift to Phase Three.

64. Permission is not granted.

117

LIZ: This is getting boring.

MOTIVATOR: Yeah, fine. I guess that'll work. (*then, friendly*) Sorry, I should have told you before. I'm the doctor for the little boy who's dying.

LIZ: He is dying!

MOTIVATOR: Yes. And the only thing that will cure him is if he wins the student-council election.

LIZ: That makes sense.

MOTIVATOR: The thing is, it won't work if you tell anyone, even his parents. Do you understand?

(*Sirens in the distance*)

LIZ: Sure. Don't tell anybody.

MOTIVATOR: Even his parents. Or you'll kill—

(*Sirens get much louder*)

MOTIVATOR: Are those coming here?

LIZ: You set off the alarm when you opened the window.

(*Beat of silence*)

MOTIVATOR: I hate you.

(*Sound of steel-toed boots scrambling out a window*)

LIZ: Bye! Thanks for the pictures!

(*Fin*)

Chapter 15:
EVIL IS MADE, NOT BORN

I am not purely a force for destruction. I don't only produce electro-rays, untraceable poisons, and blackmail files. One time, for instance, I invented this *amazing* gold-plated back scratcher—I think I already mentioned it. I also sometimes publish counterfeit Archie comics, in which Betty and Veronica dump that idiot Archie and devote their lives to worshipping the great Reggie. Because I think there's an audience for that.

But if I don't make more *constructive* contributions to society, it's really not my fault. I've never gotten any encouragement for such ventures.

When I was five, my family drove to Florida for a week's vacation. My father's friend Don owned a house down there.

I spent most of my first day at the beach building a sand castle with Mom, while Daddy sat in a folding chair reading (*see plate 11*). For the most part, it was like he wasn't even on the same vacation with us. He just sat there, reading, wearing black sunglasses and a blue Chicago Cubs baseball cap, getting bright red streaks on

PLATE 11: I spent most of my first day at the beach
building a sand castle

his shoulders.[65] But at one point, he looked up from his book and gave our castle a surprised look.

"Wow, Marlene," he said. "That's some castle."

"Ollie did most of it," she said proudly.

"Well, what do you know" he said. "Huh." He sounded genuinely, almost kind of impressed. He got up and walked around the castle slowly, getting down on his knees to examine a particularly cunning parapet. "Good work, Ollie." He turned to "Mom." "Maybe he'll grow up to be an architect. Sometimes the ones who have the worst verbal skills have the best spatial abilities."

---

65. His fault. He'd complained when "Mom" smeared sunblock on him.

"He has wonderful verbal skills," said "Mom." "He just doesn't talk very much."

It is hard for me to describe the delighted tingle that was running through my body all through this conversation. Probably because it's the only time in my life I've *felt* that tingle. God help me, it's probably what Lollipop feels when I tell her, "Good dog."

How sick is that? I was five—way old enough to know better, and yet some small part of me still wanted to please this sunburned buffoon. I guess boys are hardwired to admire their fathers. But when I look back at this weakness in my five-year-old self, I get almost physically ill. Thank God, I'm over *that*.

After making his proud noises, Daddy went back to his book. Then the tide started to come in, inching ever closer to my castle walls. So I got busy with my plastic shovel. I am not the first child who ever started digging a moat around his castle to try to save it from the oncoming waves.

"Time to go, son," said Daddy.

"I'm not finished."
"You're just digging holes."

I smiled up at him. "I'm keeping the water from wrecking my castle."

"Oh, Ollie," said Mom. She looked heartbroken. "The ocean washes away *everyone's* sand castles. I'm so *sorry*, honey."

But I kept digging. My father smiled at her and whispered, "Let him finish. It's a good lesson for him to learn. There are some things he can't control."

My mother rummaged in her bag to find me a cookie.

It took me about ten more minutes to finish digging my network of trenches, pits, and grooves in the sand.

Then we went back to Don's house and ate corned-beef sandwiches for dinner.

I woke up early the next day. I couldn't wait to go back to the water. I wanted to feel that tingle again.[66]

When we got to the beach, Daddy spent a few minutes setting his chair up, laying his towel down, rubbing aloe vera on his shoulders. Then he finally looked around, surveying the shoreline like some all-powerful fairy-tale king. That's when he noticed my castle, twenty yards away.
It was pristine. Perfect. It had not been touched by a single wave.

Mom was very happy for me and immediately suggested we add a giant tower to the center. But my eyes were on

66. I taste vomit as I write these words. *Vomit.*

Daddy. He didn't say anything for a while. He walked around the castle again, like he'd done the day before, examining it even more closely. Like he wanted to see if it was really the same castle.

I suppose I was expecting him to say, "Wow, Ollie." Or, "Good work, son." I would have settled for "Good dog."

What he said was, "What the hell? . . . " And when he finally looked at me, what I saw wasn't justifiable paternal pride. His skinny little lips had gone transparent from the blood fleeing his face. His nostrils were wide as half-dollars, like a gorilla smelling gunpowder. His beady eyes were narrowed into greedy, suspicious slits.

What I saw was fear. Horror. He was *threatened* by me.

Here I had devised an entirely new system of hydraulic engineering—out of sand—a system that could easily keep the world's coastlines safe from hurricanes, typhoons, and whatever other nonsense nature throws at us—and my father's reaction was not only *disbelief*, it was *disgust. Terror.*

He was scared I would somehow *surpass* him. As much as he might moan about what a disappointment his dumb son was, his ego couldn't tolerate a son who might be *better* than him.

That's when I realized I was destined to either disappoint my father or terrify him. There would be no middle ground, no soft and squishy place called "pride."

But that's also when I realized I didn't care.[67] I still don't. I don't need his approval. I don't need his love. I don't need anything. I've got my genius to keep me warm. And I certainly don't need to *build* anything to prove myself to him.

Daddy settled back into his chair and started reading again, after saying something about "a fluke" and "a-one-in-a-billion chance."

I kicked the castle down and spent the rest of the day breaking seashells.

And that's pretty much what I've done every day since.

---

67. Okay, I know I made it sound like I decided not to care about my father when I was a baby, but this was the moment when I *really* realized I didn't care about him. Permanently.

Chapter 16:
I DRAW A HISTORICAL PARALLEL

In 1936, a German company completed construction of the LZ 129 *Hindenburg*. The *Hindenburg* was a zeppelin—basically, a blimp with an ego. It was as big as the *Titanic*, but it flew.

Unfortunately, not for long. In 1937, as it was coming in for a landing, the *Hindenburg* burst into flames, killing thirty-six people and two dogs (*see plate 12*). A radio reporter on the scene was so moved by the carnage, he started spouting some of the best poetry ever spoken over American airwaves: "It's smoke and it's flames now . . . and the frame is crashing to the ground, not quite to the mooring mast . . . Oh, the humanity!"[68]

Although nothing was ever proved, there has always been speculation that what happened to the *Hindenburg* wasn't an accident. It was the biggest, most famous thing that has ever flown—and when you are that big, that famous, you are bound to make enemies.[69]

---

68. He cursed a lot, too, but they never play that part on the radio.

69. It didn't help that Hitler—the creep with the moustache—insisted it be decorated with swastikas. He had *lots* of enemies.

PLATE 12: In 1937, as it was coming in for a landing, the *Hindenburg* burst into flames, killing 36 people and two dogs.

Which is why cover has always been so important to me. Why I've done everything I can to fly under the radar at school, to be a being of complete bland boringness to my

classmates. When you draw attention to yourself, dangerous things can happen.

For instance: Liz Twombley is hugging me. Furiously. Frantically. Right in the middle of the cafeteria. Her left hand clasps the back of my head and grinds my face into her body. Since Liz stands a good foot taller than me, even you can do this math.[70] I am caught in a web of equal parts humiliation and exhilaration.

"Oh, Oliver," she emotes. "You'll be the best class president ever." Her clique—Megan Polanski, Shiri O'Doul, and Rashida Grant—remain seated at the Popular Table, watching this display with abject, slack-jawed horror. I struggle to free myself, but I can't decide how hard I should fight.

"Be careful, Crisco-breath," taunts Tatiana, sauntering past with a carton of chocolate milk. "You might suffocate."

That makes up my mind for me. I somehow find the strength to push Liz away, find the appropriate words to say thank you ("Your sweater smells fuzzy"), and rush to my table, where Randy Sparks waits with a slice of pizza—forgotten—stuck halfway into his mouth.

Liz gives me one last longing look and returns to her friends. Megan, Shiri, and Rashida, without speaking, without exchanging so much as a glance or gesture, stand up and move to another table. Middle-school cruelty has struck again. The girl who took me into her arms was the Most Popular Girl in School. The girl who let me go is nothing.

Liz is just one of the victims of my political career. This

---

70. The maternal instinct is strong in this one.

morning, Jack Chapman announced he was withdrawing from the race so he could concentrate on his studies.[71]

There's also been a massive increase in farting in class. My new high profile has made me a magnet for bullies, even bullies who should know better, and I suspect Pistol, Bardolph, and Nym are running low on blow-darts. Yesterday, Alan Pitt—he of the loud mouth and bad complexion—slammed me into a locker so hard I nearly broke a finger. My minions filled him with Lazopril darts, but too late to do any good. Ten minutes later, he laid such a stinker in history class that I thought the gas was going to melt the zits off his face.

Still, it's all worth it. Once again, I have triumphed.

Randy Sparks has recovered enough to swallow the cheese in his mouth. He gives me an encouraging smile. "I guess you're going to be president now, Ollie."

I dig frantically into my pocket and pull out a greasy dollar bill. I push it across the table to him. "Okay, okay. Here," I say. "It's all I've got."

Randy is puzzled. "I don't want your money."

"It's all I've got!" I scream, "I'll bring more tomorrow!"

---

71. At least that kind of makes sense. Liz announced she was dropping out so she "could spend more time with [her] family."

He gives me a nervous smile, looks around to see who's heard me. "No. Take it back. That's yours."

"*Okay*! *Okay*! I'll steal money from my Mommy and give it to you!"

"But I don't want—" Randy is yanked to his feet by the beefy paw of Miss Broadway, a rather enormous new math teacher. "Leave him alone," she commands.

"But I wasn't—I don't want his money. I don't know why he thought—" protests Randy, but the look on Broadway's broad face silences him.

"Really, Rudy, I expect better from you."

"Randy," says Randy miserably.

"Whatever you're calling yourself today," says Broadway, refusing to concede anything. "Now move to another table. And if I see you bothering Oliver again, I'll report you."

Randy sighs[72] and walks out of the cafeteria, leaving his lunch behind. Maybe I've pushed him a little too hard this time. But nuisances like Randy Sparks shouldn't be encouraged, and since there's no way I can apologize, I do the next best thing and finish his pizza for him.

---

72. It's his signature sound.

Coincidentally, it's pizza night at the Watson house (Mom burned her tuna soufflé), and we are all digging into a large pie from Big Fred's.

Daddy is nibbling at his half of the pie, which is covered with pepperoni (which I find repulsive). "So," he asks, trying to muster up something that resembles excitement, "how's the campaign going?"

I've waited patiently through his entire dinnertime lecture (tonight's topic: "Let's make the politicians fight the wars!") for him to give me this opening.

"I'm president," I say, through a mouth full of anchovies and hot peppers.

Daddy makes his obligatory attempt to contradict me. "No, you have to be elected first."

And this is where I get to drop my bomb.

"Nuh-uh, Daddy. Liz and Jack dropped out, so I'm the only one running." I speak slowly, both to savor the moment and to make sure he hears me right. "So I get to be president. Just like you."

The entire point of dropping a bomb is to get an explosion. Mom obliges, and is out of her seat and hugging me,

Twombley style, in no time flat. But that's not the explosion I wanted.

My eyes are on Daddy, who sits there, eyes unfocused, fondling his glasses, looking concerned. Confused. What bitter truths must be racing through his brain right now? What new, grudging respect for his only son is forcing its way onto his consciousness? His mouth opens. Here it comes. Here it comes....

"I'm sorry, Oliver."

No.

He should be staring down at his plate, rethinking his entire youth, realizing just how empty his school-age accomplishments were, since *I* can equal them.

Or he should be looking at me with admiration. With realization. He should be slapping me on the back, giving me a proud and hearty "Good work, kid." Not that I want that.

Or he should be weeping. Just weeping. Weeping would be fine.

But not *this*. Not *pity*.

"Oliver won," says Mom, confused.

"No, dear. Oliver's going to be president. But he didn't win anything," says Daddy. He gives me a rueful smile—the one that means he's about to teach me a very important lesson. "I think Oliver knows what I'm talking about."

For once in his life, Oliver doesn't have a clue.

"We live in a *democracy*." He says the word like it's something holy. "And the important thing in a democracy isn't *winning* an election—it's *participating* in it. The struggle. The campaign. I mean, if you just *walk into* the office, well . . . it's wonderful to be so valued by your peers"—here he gives me a condescending wink—"but really, you haven't won anything, have you? It's like something you'd see in a Communist country. Or some banana republic where the elections are fixed. Would my victory in tenth grade have been as sweet if I hadn't had to beat Louis Goldberg? It wouldn't have been a victory at all.

"The beauty of the American system is the crucible of ideas. Two people—or more—being thrown into the ring and having to win the hearts and minds of their fellow citizens. That's what keeps government strong. And that's what keeps *student* government strong."

I think my heart has stopped beating.

My God. He actually believes this crap. And, in his eyes, I have accomplished *nothing*.

Does he think Rocket-Firing Boba Fett Dolls grow on trees?

He's convinced one member of his audience. "I'm sorry, Oliver," says Mom. "I didn't understand.... Maybe you'll get to run against somebody next year." She gives me her most loving smile.

Daddy gives me a playful punch on the shoulder. "I guess it just wasn't meant to be, huh, Champ?"

I nod, and I try to swallow, but it feels like I'm swallowing chalk dust. I can feel my features hardening into a permanently blank mask. *What do I have to do to impress this man?*[73]

I tap my left foot once....

My internal organs are melting together—I can feel them—congealing into a stew of red-hot lava. They threaten to spew out my mouth and all over his rotten smirk.

I tap my left foot again....

I can feel my hair turning into freezing cold fire. It's drilling into my brain.

I tap my left foot a third time....

"Why is she doing that?" sweats Daddy.

---

73. Not that I care.

He's looking down at Lolli, who is glaring up at him with hate like he's never seen before. She sounds like she swallowed a chain saw. Her nostrils are wide and foaming. Her eyes are as flat and dead as two dirty pennies.

"She needs a walk," I say.

"She just went out before dinner," says Mom.

"She needs a walk," I say, and I jump to my feet. My faithful hound, my loving, loyal dog follows me out the door.

Lollipop needs a walk? *I* need a walk.

I need to let my temper cool before I accidentally tap my left foot a fourth and final time—and Lollipop does something neither of us can take back.

And more than that: I need an opponent.

Chapter 17:
I AM IN A FOUL MOOD

Do you like video games?

Of course, you do.

Come here. You'll *love* this one.

You know the game where you have a plastic guitar, and you hit buttons that make the little guitarist on screen strum along to whatever song is playing? This is like that game but better.

I am sitting in the amphitheater, a part of my Control Center I don't use much. I am playing with a plastic guitar. There's a thick curtain in the center of the room. My technicians are getting the game ready behind that curtain.

"We're done, sir," says Chauncey the technician (who's been much more respectful lately).

"Excellent. Let's begin!"

Chauncey pulls back the heavy velvet curtain, revealing two stacks of the largest stereo amplifiers you will ever see in your life. There's a marionette hanging in the air between them. What's interesting about this marionette is that it is a real person. A fourteen-year-old boy, in fact, in a pair of *Knight Rider* pajamas. There's a bag over his head.

And one more thing: There's a guitar strapped to his chest.

"Bag off," I order. A technician pulls a string, and the bag is yanked into the rafters. Oh, look—the marionette is actually Alan Pitt! I'm surprised the bag fit over his zits.

"Hi, Alan!" I say, perfectly friendly. "What do you want to play first?"

"Who is that?" says Alan, who is still wearing a blindfold. "Where am I? What's going on?"

"We're having a playdate. What kind of music do you like? You a classic-rock guy? You look like a classic-rock guy."

He turns his flabby pink ear toward me. "I know that voice. You go to school with me. Who is this? Parker Albanese? Because I flushed your iPod down the toilet?"

"No..." I drawl slowly. The tension in the air is delicious.

"Randy Sparks? Because I peed in your gym locker? I will crush you for this. ..."

"Maybe..."

"Ted Philips? You only *thought* I kicked your ass last time. That was just a warm-up. Or maybe that fat kid who drinks chocolate pudding through a straw. I spit in your hair one time. Did you know that?"

I decide to play Cream's "Tales of Brave Ulysses"[74] first. I really love Clapton's guitar work on that song, even though pretty much everything he's done since then gives me diarrhea.[75]

As the first quiet, spooky notes creep out of the speakers, and Jack Bruce starts singing about "shiny purple fishes," my fingers delicately touch the buttons on my controller. The ropes tied to the marionette jerk into action, forcing him to gently strum the guitar.

"What...hey...this is..."

---

74. Man does not live by Beefheart alone.

75. I will also overlook the misuse of the epithet *brave* to describe Ulysses. Look at the *Odyssey*—he's always called "sly Ulysses," never "brave Ulysses." I respect him for that, by the way. Any idiot can be brave.

Ginger Baker's drumsticks CRACK down like the Auction Hammer of God, and Eric Clapton begins an almost ugly pounding stomp down an endless guitar staircase. My little fingers sweat on the buttons as I try to keep up.

The marionette is doing some *really* impressive stuff now—bobbing, jerking, strumming, kicking, windmilling.

Once, when I've hit enough notes in a row, the marionette goes into a split, ripping his pajamas.

"Ow! Who's *doing* this? Just *stop*!" That's the marionette talking. It keeps saying those things, no matter what buttons I push. Maybe if I play long enough . . .

Sheldrake joins me halfway through "Sweet Jane." I turn down the music so we can hear each other. Lollipop, who's curled up on top of my bare feet, whines with appreciation; she's wearing special noise-canceling earphones I devised for her, but I know they don't keep out all the sound.

"You want a go?" I ask.

Sheldrake glances at the marionette. "Not to criticize, but you're torturing a child."

I snort. "He's taller than you are. Heavier, too."

But he shakes his head. "Nah, I'm no good at video games. Congratulations, by the way."

"On what?"

"On the election."

"It's not over yet." My fingers slide across the sweat-slick buttons.

"What do you mean?"

"Daddy says I can't win without an opponent."

"Oh," says Sheldrake. "When did he—"

"Tonight."

Sheldrake looks at me funny. Then he looks at the marionette funny.

"I'm gonna get you—ow! I'll make you sorry—ow!" threatens the marionette, as he does a double somersault.

Sheldrake puts a hand on my shoulder. "Maybe you should play this game when you're a little less"—he searches for the right words—"*on edge.*"

"But I feel like playing it now."

He reaches for the controller. "I've changed my mind about playing."

But I won't give it to him. "I've changed my mind about sharing."

I'm a fan of Lynyrd Skynyrd, too. Their songs are full of brutal, punishing guitar solos. I end up playing every track on their first three albums.

Chapter 18:
WHAT ARE YOU LOOKING AT, BUTTHEAD?

Sorry. I just felt like saying that.

I sleep a lot in class. It's sort of expected of me. Nobody ever seems to wonder why dumb children are so much sleepier than smart ones. It all depends on the dumb child in question. Some of them have chores to do, or younger siblings to take care of, or crappy parents who fight all the time and won't let them sleep. Some of them are true morons who stay up all night watching TV. And some of them burn the midnight oil, running secret global empires.

Most teachers are happy to let their worst students sleep, so that their better students can learn. Not Lucy Sokolov.

She's jabbing me with a yardstick. That's the first of my senses to be engaged—I *feel* the yardstick in my ribs. Then I *hear* the baboons around me laughing, and Sokolov's vinegar-thin voice above the din: "Wake up. Now." When I open my eyes, I see Tatiana, skewed sideways, smirking down at me from her desk.

But that's significant: She's smirking, not laughing. Not like the animals. I *smell* her sweet, cheap aroma— fabric softener, bubble gum, and ChapStick; it wraps itself around me, sends its scented fingers down my throat. Suddenly, I can *taste* the saliva in my mouth, alkaline and hungry. And I'm reminded of why I'm so hungry in the first place.

Then Sokolov walks between us and ruins it all.[76] "Face off the desk," she orders. I comply with a bare-thigh-on-vinyl *rip* (some of the saliva has leaked from my mouth). She pulls out her roll book. "Watson, Oliver," she reads. "Here."

I hate study hall.

Randy Sparks, the Most Pathetic Boy in School, is sharpening a pencil. Sokolov gives him a quick glance, then gives him an abrupt order: "Randy Sparks. Please go to the front of the room."

When she says "please," it sounds wet and bloody, like somebody clubbing a baby seal to death.

Randy gives her a puzzled look, then, eager to please as ever, walks to the front of the room and turns to face the class. He has a strange, hopeful smile on his face. What could this be about?

---

76. She smells like soap and herbal tea.

Ms. Sokolov says, "Your fly is unzipped."

Everyone in the room stops looking at Randy's face and starts looking at his crotch. His fly isn't just unzipped—it's *gaping*. And the tighty-whities he's wearing don't look very clean, either. His fingers fumble as they yank his stubborn zipper back up. Now our eyes go back to his face. He's blushing so badly it looks like someone has dipped his head in the stuff they use to make red candy apples. The smile is still on his lips, frozen there, but now it is the saddest, most hopeless smile on earth.

He honestly looks like he might cry. He is having a very hard time deciding not to—

Then the bell rings and he rushes out the door. I feel like sprinting out myself—but I get stuck in my chair for the briefest of moments, and by the time I extricate myself, Tatiana is blocking the door. She leans negligently against the wall like some B-movie villain, picking at the electric-pink spackle on her left thumbnail. She doesn't bother to look at me.

"Going somewhere, Fats?"

"Geometry."

"Forget geometry. You're going to the top, Tubby. The top." She points her remarkably razor-sharp chin in my direction. "I'm glad it worked out for you. Too bad my little trick didn't do it."

I goggle at her. What trick is she talking about?

She rewards me with a sneaky smile. "See, I'm like your secret campaign manager. I'm the one who told everybody you were dying. So they'd vote for you, see?"

Ah! So it was Tatiana who started that rumor! I should've known! My classmates are far too feebleminded to come up with such an ingenious story without some mastermind pushing them in the right direction. Little gears in my head start clicking into place—no wonder she'd been so gleeful when everyone else felt bad for me.

She pauses, reconsiders. "Actually, I only told three people. They told everybody else. That's how rumors work."

Even for Tatiana, this is impressive. Few middle-school students have such an advanced understanding of the art of rumor spreading.

I dart a worried glance at Sokolov, who sits at the front of the room with her nose buried in a book.[77] Tati follows my gaze. "You think that thing over there cares what we talk about?"

I'm impressed by her ability to dehumanize *La Sokolova*.

---

77. She has a free period but doesn't go to the teachers lounge anymore.

"She's probably your favorite teacher."

"What? 'Cause she's so nasty? Nah." Tati wrinkles her nose. "She's nothing. Just a broken sofa spring that sticks through the cushion. It makes you bleed when you sit on it, but not 'cause it wants to. It's just what it *is*. She ain't mean. She's just broken."

Tatiana has raised her voice significantly for this summation. Maybe "that thing over there" doesn't care about what we're saying, but I notice its eyes are glowing behind the book.
Tatiana blows confetti off her thumbnail. "Just know—I'm watching you."

I manage to stammer out a "Wh-why?"

This time she blows the confetti in my face. "Because nobody's as dumb as you act."

Two things occur to me as I rush to geometry, five minutes late:
• Tatiana is very perceptive.
• I owe her a pair of sunglasses.

I squeeze into my seat in geometry as Miss Broadway glares at me. Time to set my latest Great Evil Plan in motion. Step One: *Set up a Chump to Run Against Me for President.*

I glance over to see what Randy's doing, but it looks like he's skipping class today. I guess he's waiting for the humiliation to wear off.

There's a folder waiting for me, taped to the underside of my desk. I pull it out and start reading. It's a hastily gathered Probe on Scott Sparks, the Most Pathetic Accountant in Omaha (*see plate 13*).

Barely graduated from a bad college. Barely hired by a bad accounting firm. Barely tolerated by his co-workers. No chance for promotion. No social life. Wife left him five years ago. One son.

Sparks and son live in a small rented house on Dundee Boulevard. The lawn is dying, and the interior photos taken by my Research Minion (who was posing as an exterminator) depict the very depths of lower middle-class hell. Dust everywhere. Abandoned pop bottles and pizza crusts on every flat surface. Towers of file folders and remnants of the just-passed tax season fill half the floor space, and the Sparks men must walk through the narrow caverns created by them just to get to the bathroom (*see plate 14*).

One bright spot: the shiny, top-of-the-line dirt bike Scott bought his son for Christmas. Randy rides it for hours after school. Scott always tells him to bring the bike inside when he's done for the night, but more often than not, Randy

**PLATE 13: Scott Sparks,
the Most Pathetic Accountant in Omaha.**

PLATE 14: Interior photos taken by my Research Minion
depict the very depths of lower middle-class hell.

just leans it against the front of the house. People are frequently careless with the things they love most.

The dad and the dirt bike. Those are my points of entry.

I'm studying these photos, formulating a plan, when a massive shadow envelops me. "What are you looking at, Oliver?" demands Miss Broadway, glowering.

I'm getting very tired of teachers sneaking up on me.

"Nothing," I say, and start to close the file, but she is not to be put off so easily. "Let me see that." She thrusts her hamlike hands at me.

"Fire drill," I murmur. Instantly, the alarm goes off, and Broadway has much more important things on her mind.

And, quite frankly, so do I.

Chapter 19:
NEWS FLASHES

Excerpted from "Famed Political Operative Retires to Omaha,"[78] *Omaha World-Herald*, April 22:

[S]he is probably best known for the "Why Does His Wife Look Scared?" commercial she created for the 2004 Democratic presidential primary. Leaders from both sides of the aisle roundly condemned the ad when it appeared, but her services were once again in high demand, by both parties, for the 2005 congressional races....

[Salisbury], who has no previous connection to Omaha, says she "simply fell in love" with the modest Dundee Dell neighborhood on a trip through the Midwest. "I saw a house I wanted and decided to stay," she says from the porch of her...

...are baffled. "I've known Verna for fifteen years. This doesn't make any sense at all," says one source who asked

---

78. Call this Part Two of my Great Evil Plan: *Hire Someone to Run (and Ruin) The Chump's Campaign.*

to remain anonymous. "She loves the game. She loves running political campaigns. She loves taking some loser and getting him elected." But Salisbury says she's "sick of all that" and, even though, at age thirty-seven, she's at the height of her career and earning potential, her next goal is to "find someone special" to spend her life with....

Excerpted from "Don't Be Bad or You Will Have Bad Dreams" by Alan Pitt, *The Gale Sayers Middle School Trumpet*, Spring Issue:

[S]ometimes even when your doing something you think is fun, like maybe making somebody suck on your gym sock, in your brain you know that really you shouldn't be doing that. You wil feel bad later and it will make you have bad dreams.

[T]he dreams can be so scary you will wake up the next day all bruised and tired and your pajamas are ripped. You will think the dream was a real thing that happened! Until your parents take you to a sykiatrist who tells you it was just a dream.

Don't be bad! ...In conclusion, as much fun as it is to smear your boogers on some little kid's face, it is not worth the bad dreams.

Excerpted from "Deposed Dictator Vows Revenge," *West African Gazette,* **April 24:**

[H]e escaped in a helicopter when his palace was stormed by democratic revolutionaries in last week's coup. He retains control of bank accounts worth an estimated eight billion dollars, though he was forced to leave several of his most valued possessions behind, including his famous collection of *Star Wars* action figures.

["A]ny aggressive move on his part will be swiftly, completely, and devastatingly countered," said the newly elected president, who added that his government is keeping a close eye on the recently deposed strongman.

[T]he former despot spoke belligerently from the throne room of his court in exile in Basel, Switzerland. "I *know* who did this to me...."

Chapter 20:
"MEET CUTE"

A photo essay featuring:

Randy Sparks, the Most Pathetic Boy in School;

Scott Sparks, the Most Pathetic Accountant in Omaha;

Operatives 11, 52, 53, and 108;

and introducing—Verna Salisbury!

PHOTO 1: A beloved dirt bike is carelessly left unguarded!

PHOTO 2: A Black Ops team extracts the bike.

PHOTO 3: "Oh, woe! My bike is stolen!"
The theft is reported to the proper authorities.

PHOTO 4: Meanwhile, in a dark and dirty alley, the bike is given to a mysterious woman.

PHOTO 5: "Excuse me, sir. Is this your lost bike? I wrestled it from a team of ruffians."

PHOTO 6: Joy! Boy and bike are reunited!
"Thank you, Madame, for returning my son's toy.
How can I repay you?"
"You can start by taking me to dinner."
Love is in the air!

Chapter 21:
LOVE IS IN THE AIR

Traditionally, the most effective way to stop a pair of cats from mating[79] is to turn a garden hose on them. It causes them no lasting harm, while ending the disgusting yowling they make while doing it. Plus, it ends the threat of unwanted kittens.

Kwame Kirkland and Cheri Munson are kissing in the hallway, and they couldn't care less who sees them. Kwame is tall and almost old enough to shave. Cheri is short and could probably get pregnant. They're in eighth grade, so I guess they think they're grown-ups now. What they actually are is a repulsive two-person sound machine that makes a slurping noise you can hear from five feet away.

Once I'm safely past them, I mutter, "Sprinkler malfunction, sector fifteen." The slurping instantly stops, replaced by the much more pleasant pitter-patter of water spraying from the ceiling and the squealing complaints of Kwame and Cheri. Animals and people—not so very different after all.

---

79. Or fighting. Pretty much the same thing with cats.

I'm brought up short by a sharp pain in my side. I look down for its cause and see a sharp brown elbow attached to a short brown girl. "Jeez, Jumbo," says Tati. "How thick is your stomach, anyway? I had to poke you like five times to get your attention."

"Mudlark," I mutter.

"Mudlark, to you too," says Tatiana. "Listen, I got good news. The campaign is in full swing."

"I already won," I tell her. "I'm the only one running." Soon that won't be true—but I'm the only one at school who knows that.

Tatiana wrinkles her perfect, pert nose and pushes her pink plastic bangles up her arm. "You can never be too careful," she says. "Politics is tricky. But don't worry, I'm getting out the vote for you. Look!"

She points down the hallway. Logan Michaels, her slave, stands by the cafeteria door, looking miserable. Liz Twombley, the ex–Most Popular Girl in School, stands next to her, looking delighted. They're both wearing cheap white T-shirts that read TEAM TUBBY. Underneath these words is a drawing of a snowman—you know, three circles stuck on top of each other.

"Vote for Oliver," says Logan, with real sadness in her voice, to the mob pushing its way into the lunchroom.

"Vote for Oliver!" says Liz, all sunshine and light.

"You like?" says Tati. "I designed those shirts myself."

"They're pretty," I say. Liz sees us and smiles. "Hi Oliver! Don't die!"

"I won't."

Liz beams like I just gave her a pony. Up close, I can see that the snowman is supposed to be me. "Thanks, Tati," I say.

"No, thank *you*," she says. "This is the most fun I've ever had at school." Then she pushes her way into the throng, taking french fries, cookies—whatever she wants—off of other peoples' trays. Laws do not apply to Nature's nobility.

Randy Sparks is sitting at my table, looking distracted. There's a strawberry fruit roll-up hanging out of his mouth that he's forgotten to finish eating.[80] I sit down and pull out my fluffernutter, but he doesn't notice I'm there.

I get it. He has a lot on his mind. His dad has a girlfriend, for one thing. That's crazy. Especially because Verna is

---

80. I know. He does that a lot.

smart and beautiful and successful. Even weirder, she wants Randy to do the *craziest* thing.[81]

And I know all this because I'm the one who's paying Verna to date Randy's dad. I'm the one who *really* wants him to do the crazy thing

"Hi, Randy."

It takes him a second to process this—it's the only time in our entire career as lunchmates I've ever said hello to him first. And one of the few times I haven't acted completely terrified of him. But I want to get a gauge of his mental state.

"Oh. Hi, Ollie," he says, finally. The fruit roll-up falls to the floor. He doesn't notice.

"Randy, do you think they'll let me be a policeman?"

"Who?" says Randy.

"When I grow up. Do you think they'll let me be one?"

His hands fiddle nervously with his lunch bag. Randy's pencil-thin forearms are covered with downy hair, and a lot of it. It's like baby hair. "I guess so," he says. "I don't see why not. I didn't know you wanted to be a policeman."

---

81. You guessed it—Step Three of the Great Evil Plan: *Get the Chump to Run.*

"I don't," I say, "but they better let me."

He doesn't have anything to say to that.
"Randy, what do you want to be when you grow up?"

His hands get more nervous. "I don't know," he says. "My dad's an accountant."

I make my eyes as big and impressed as they can be. "Wow," I say. "A Naccountant! Is he happy?"

Randy doesn't say anything for a while. He looks inside his lunch bag and seems confused that it's empty. "I don't know," he says. "Probably not." Then he adds, quickly, "He has a girlfriend."

"Wow!" I say. "Is she a policeman?"

Randy looks at me funny. I'm pushing the dumb act a little farther than usual, and he may be noticing. Then he shrugs and lets his eyes take a tour of the room. They linger on Pammy Quattlebaum, who's telling a loud nerd story to her loud nerd friends. Then he looks at Jack Chapman, who sits nearby with his buddies, flicking paper "footballs" through one another's fingers. They're all laughing at some joke. He looks at Rashida Grant, who's talking into a cell phone she snuck into school. Megan and Shiri are using their bodies to shield her from Coach Anicito, who's on lunch duty today and'll take the phone away if he sees it.

Randy looks back inside his paper bag, then he crumples it up and pushes it away. "When I grow up," he says, "I guess...well...I just want to be *normal*."

There's a conversation killer if ever I've heard one.

"Oh," I say. "Good luck with that."

"Thanks," he says. Then he gets up without saying good-bye and walks out to the school yard.

I watch him go, with a curious emotion in my chest. Is it possible for me to feel guilt?

No.

Thank God!

Chapter 22:

I WILL STAND ATHWART THIS GLOBE LIKE A TERRIFYING COLOSSUS AND I WILL STEP ON YOU IF YOU TRY TO LOOK UP MY SHORTS

Moorhead's latest cigarette reads CARRY A COPY OF *GRAVITY'S RAINBOW*. He stares at it with alarm.

I don't really blame him. Lest you forget, receiving mysterious messages on cigarettes is a pretty alarming proposition, any way you look at it.

Plus, this message tells him to carry a copy of *Gravity's Rainbow*, Thomas Pynchon's legendarily unreadable novel. Eight hundred pages long. Dense, wordy, kooky. Exactly the sort of thing to impress a smarty-pants like Lucy Sokolov, but a daunting prospect for a tiny brain like Moorhead.[82]

But I guess the most alarming thing about this particular cigarette is *where* he found it: inside an orange he just peeled. That was childish of me.

There he stands, in the middle of the hallway, slack-jawed. Ripped-open orange in one hand, pulp-covered cigarette

---

82. Note that I didn't tell him to actually *read* the book.

in the other, getting jostled by the class-bound hordes. He turns warily in a circle, scanning the vicinity for someone—a magician, perhaps? A playful god?—who could have done this. But there's only me. And I'm scratching my butt with my pencil case.

Vice Principal Hruska storms past, mentally calculating the number of seconds until he can retire. He plucks the cigarette from Moorhead's fingers. "Not on school property, Neil."

Moorhead points urgently as Hruska walks away, "Wait! Read it...."

But Hruska has already crushed the cigarette in his hand and dropped the soggy shreds in a garbage can. "Read what?"

Moorhead stares at the old man, then at the garbage, then back at the old man.

"Read what, Neil?"

Moorhead turns and walks silently back to his classroom, letting the orange slip from his limp fingers. It's like he's forgotten he was holding it.

See, not everyone likes surprises. Some people love 'em; some people have heart attacks. It's a matter of taste.

Does Randy Sparks, the Most Pathetic Boy in School, like surprises? Let's find out.[83]

He's put up with some pretty surprising stuff lately. Like his father getting a girlfriend. And it's all happened so fast! Wasn't it just a few days ago that she returned Randy's bike? After single-handedly taking it away from the motorcycle gang that stole it?

Kind of hard to believe when you think about it, but when Verna starts talking, it all makes sense. She can be very convincing—about almost anything, if the price is right. Not that Randy knows that.

The thing he mostly hears her be convincing about is the beauty of the democratic process (she used to run campaigns for *national elections*). As it turns out (and, I'll grant you, this is improbable), the elections she's really interested in now are middle-school ones. They are, apparently, incredibly important in shaping the character of "our next generation of leaders."

Naturally, Verna was horrified when Randy told her that a boy was running unopposed for the eighth-grade class presidency. Boy, was she ever horrified. She tried to convince Randy to be horrified, too, but even the Most Pathetic Boy in School isn't going to fall for that one.

---

83. This is what's known as a *segue*.

So she focused her powers of convinction on Scott Sparks, the Luckiest Man in Omaha, and he was instantly, thoroughly, completely convinced. He told his son he should run for class president. And I mean he *really* told him. Scott Sparks practically begged Randy to run for class president.

Randy didn't want to screw things up for his dad, so he promised he'd try. And, being the sort of person who keeps promises, he went to Mr. Pinckney, who said, "No, no. Absolutely not," just like Randy knew he would. And that was that. And Randy was relieved. He'd done his best.

What Randy didn't know was that one minute after he left Mr. Pinckney's office, The Motivator went into it. That was yesterday.

Today is today, and Randy and I are sitting three desks away from each other in Earth sciences. Miss Broadway teaches it. She's technically a math teacher, but because she's new, she gets stuck with a lot of the classes no one else wants. "Dirt for Dummies" is one of those classes. Right now she's talking about the big news in the science world—the burglary last night at the National Air and Space Museum in Washington.

"Thank goodness they didn't take more,[84] but *still*. I mean, *really*. This is the home of some of our most valued national

---

84. The thieves only stole two small pieces of Moon rock.

treasures. People shouldn't be able to just stroll in and take whatever they *want*."

Broadway seems less concerned with what was stolen than she is with the whole decline-in-law-and-order aspect of the story. Most of her conversations turn in this direction. In geometry, she once made a compelling speech linking the sides of a scalene triangle to a recent outburst of gang violence.

I can assure her (but I won't) that the burglars didn't "just stroll" into the museum. This was a precision military operation, conducted by top-flight Armenian mercenaries. They were in and out in under five minutes, and they didn't leave a trace.[85]

I glance at the wall clock, then over at Randy, who is picking wax out of his ear. If my instructions are being followed, just about now The Motivator is walking into Principal Pinckney's office with a little brown box.

Which means that just about *now*, Pinckney, who heard about the museum robbery with a combination of excitement and dread, is opening that little box with trembling fingers.

And just about *now*, The Motivator is reminding the Principal of his side of the bargain.

---

85. Okay, that's not completely true. I had them leave one of Miley Cyrus's fingerprints just to blow the F.B.I.'s minds.

And just about *now*...

"Your attention, please." Pinckney's voice crackles over the loudspeaker. "Attention. This is your principal. Pardon the interruption. This is...is highly unusual...."

He pauses, apparently unsure how to continue. Every eye in the room is on the little speaker mounted above the blackboard, except for mine. I'm looking at somebody sitting three desks away.

"Um. Well..."

Buried in the static hissing out of the loudspeaker, you can barely hear someone whisper, "Just say it."

"Um ... Randy Sparks is now a candidate for the eighth-grade class presidency."

Then a horrible *clank* as the microphone is abruptly shut off.

Surprise!

Turns out Randy Sparks is the have-a-heart-attack type. Only he's too young to have a heart attack, so he just turns purple and starts coughing. When he recovers, Broadway is standing over him, seemingly determined to draw the truth out of him with her immense gravity.

"What are you up to, Andy?"

"Randy."

Broadway rolls her eyes. She doesn't like students who mouth off.

Randy starts sputtering, trying to make sense of it for himself. "I don't know! I asked him yesterday; he said I couldn't . . . I didn't think he'd—"

"You just *asked* Mr. Pinckney to make you a candidate?" Broadway booms, horrified. "Don't you know that there's a *procedure* you have to follow?"

"But my dad, he . . . My dad has a *girlfriend*!"

That's enough to start the orangutans on a laughing jag and Randy on another coughing fit. Broadway storms around the room, muttering, looking personally insulted. When the animals finally quiet down, she addresses us in funereal tones.

"This is just what I was talking about before. Just *exactly*. There are rules we are supposed to follow. As a society. As a nation. As a school. When those rules aren't followed— especially *here*, where you're supposed to be learning to respect them—the wheels come off the cart. They just do!" She points a sizeable index finger at Randy. "*You* were supposed to be nominated by someone." Her voice rises in pitch, speed, and passion. "*That* nomination was supposed to be seconded. Your homeroom teacher was supposed to witness it all! Where was he or she in this process? *Who is your homeroom teacher?*"

Randy shrinks down in his seat. "You are."

The animals are laughing too loud to hear the bell ending class.

My sympathies are with Randy on this one. No one should be so anonymous that his homeroom teacher doesn't know he exists.

"Spray Broadway with solution X-9," I whisper. Tomorrow, she is going to come down with a very, very bad cold.

"And solution X-5."

And a rash.

"And let the air out of her tires."

Now I'm just being nasty.

Chapter 23:
DADDY HAS OTHER THINGS ON HIS MIND

Daddy stands at his closet, combing through his collection of bow ties. I have nothing against bow ties personally, except when Daddy wears them. He likes to wear *fun* items of clothing when he gets dressed up, as if to say, *I don't take things like this too seriously*.

"What do you think?" he says, holding up two ties. "The one with dancing babies on it, or the one with rollerskating Frankensteins?" I take a special joy in giving him the stupidest ties I can find every Christmas and Father's Day. I would enjoy it even more if he didn't like them so much.

"They're both nice," says Mom, who sits on the bed. He nods, gives each tie another serious look, then puts them aside for further consideration. He's picking out what he'll wear on his station's upcoming pledge drive, a monthlong extravaganza of whining for dollars.

Daddy drops his favorite corduroy jacket on the pile, then puts a hand to his noble brow. "God, I hate this." He looks even more world-weary than usual. "Wasting my time going on air. So many important things I could be doing in my office ..."

"Then don't do it," I say, sitting on the floor, playing tug-of-war with Lollipop.[86]

Daddy looks a little too pained to respond. Mom fills the vacuum. "He has to do it, Sugarplum. He's scheduled to be on TV three nights a week. For a month!"

"Yeah," I say, drawing it out, as if the idea is just dawning on me. "But he's the boss of the whole station."

"That's right."

"So isn't he the one who makes the schedule? He could make it so other people have to go on TV, and then he can do all the *important* work in his office—"

"Someday you'll understand what it means to have responsibilities," snaps Daddy. He turns back to his closet with a passion and starts pawing through his wardrobe with real energy.

"Maybe when I beat Randy and become president," I say.

"Yeah, maybe then," says Daddy, distracted. Pledge-

---

86. I'm waiting for a certain someone to notice we're playing with his favorite T-shirt.

drive season takes up an insane amount of my parents' mental energy. He starts pawing through his sock drawer.

I thought he'd be a little more interested when he heard I had an opponent. "It's going to be a tough election," I venture. "I'm scared Randy will get all the kids who have glasses to vote for him. Because he has glasses."

My parents haven't heard a word of it. Daddy's examining a pair of bright-orange socks. "I can't wear these on TV—they're stained."

"You should get a haircut," says Mom.

He looks in the mirror. "No," he says, stroking the curls around his pointed ears. "Then it would look like I cared."

I shouldn't be surprised by their lack of enthusiasm. As it turns out, Randy Sparks's late entry in the race wasn't even the biggest news at school today. After lunch, word leaked out that Tatiana had been suspended for two weeks. Someone's been spray-painting graffiti in the parking lot since January. Typical juvenile stuff (*see plate 15*). This morning, Ms. Sokolov remembered that she'd seen paint on Tatiana's fingers the other day. And that was that.

Here's the funny thing: The vandal uses blue paint.

PLATE 15: Someone's been spray-painting graffiti in the parking lot since January. Typical juvenile stuff.

People are creatures of habit. If you picked your nose with your left pinkie finger yesterday, you'll probably pick it with your left pinkie finger today, and with your left pinkie finger tomorrow, forever and ever for the rest of your ugly snot-covered life.

Let's talk about someone much less disgusting than you: Tatiana. As far as creatures of habit go, she is probably the most habitually pink creature in the world. Her sweaters

177

are pink, her socks are pink, her sneakers are pink, her panties are pink.[87]

Even if my surveillance cameras hadn't taken photographs proving that the vandal is actually Jordie Moscowitz (he's a real winner), I would have had a very hard time believing that someone so thoroughly pink as our Tati would choose to express herself in blue. It just doesn't work that way.

On the other hand, people can embrace *new* habits when they realize their old habits just aren't *working* for them anymore. Take Moorhead, for example. He's decided to let mystical messages typed on cigarettes guide him in the pursuit of his dream woman. You might call this behavior irrational, but it's probably the most sensible thing he's done in years. He knows he's not making any progress with Sokolov on his own; if the cigarette messages offer a better path, he'd be a fool not to follow it.

Even a middle-school middlebrow like Moorhead knows why his angels have advised him to "CARRY A COPY OF *GRAVITY'S RAINBOW*." It's to make him look smart. Sokolov is bound to be impressed by a man who reads something so thick.

Which is why he looked so pleased with himself this afternoon. A copy of *Gravity's Rainbow* loomed ominously on

---

87. Or so my Research Department tells me.

the corner of his desk, like a two-ton marble monument to his brain. He was leaning back in his chair, hands clasped behind his neck, beaming like a baby that's used the potty for the first time.

Oh yes, he was thinking. *This makes me look smart.*

At one point he saw Pammy Quattlebaum eyeing the book in admiration, and he flashed her an arrogant smile, like a rock star grinning at a fan.

Meanwhile, a pack of hastily prepared cigarettes, all screaming HIDE THAT THING IN A DRAWER, were being rush-delivered to him.

It was a *brand-new* copy of the book. You'd think even a middle-school middlebrow would know better than that. How's he supposed to impress Sokolov if she thinks he's reading *Gravity's Rainbow* for the *first time*?[88]

"The next message will read GET A USED COPY," I dictate, though there's no one but Lollipop, Sheldrake, and me in the blimp. Somewhere, far beneath us, someone hears me and someone obeys.

"You're too cruel to that man," says Sheldrake.

"He doesn't think so." I scan some tax returns for errors.

---

88. That's smarty-pants rule No.1: Make it look like you've read every book *twice*.

Nothing pops up, but I can't say I'm all that interested. I push the stack of paperwork aside. "By the way, Lionel, I'm arranging a few public appearances for you."

"Do I have to?"

"One of them, you'll actually enjoy. It's on my father's station. The other . . . well, that's going to be at my school. A speech about the value of democratic elections in the public-school arena."

Sheldrake breathes heavily and fidgets in his seat. I glare at him. "Spit it out."

"You're certainly making a big deal out of this election."

"I want it to be a *very* big deal," I say. "I want people to recognize that this is important."

"You mean you want one person in particular to think it's important." I stiffen, and Lollipop shows Sheldrake all five thousand of her little white needles.

Sheldrake barrels forward, heedless. "Look, you know I never give you advice—but why do you care what *he* thinks? You're twice the man he is, and you haven't even hit puberty yet."

I grab the speaking trumpet. "Captain Malthus, open the bay

doors. We're going to be dumping something over the river."
The floor behind Sheldrake's chair collapses downward, like a horizontal pair of saloon doors in a cowboy
movie, and the white lights of the Omaha skyline bathe
us in their glow. Tax forms flap around the cabin like
bats. "*Hil*," I command, and Lollipop inches toward
Sheldrake, teeth bared, back arched.

Sheldrake pales. "There's no need to threaten me, Oliver.
I'll shut up. But I don't see why you don't just fix the
damned election and be done with it." He's being very
brave. "Just rig the vote and stop worrying about it."

Lollipop's growl rises an octave. It becomes scarier as it
becomes more shrill. She's less than a foot from him now.
The slobber that hangs from her mouth glistens in the
reflected light like a silver knife.

"Damn it, Oliver. Stop that dog."

I respect him for not saying "Please."

"*Maita*," I order. Lollipop stops, just a few inches short of him.
All the hostility instantly drains from her body. She cranes
forward and licks the sweat from Sheldrake's cheeks.

"Captain Malthus, close the bay." We cease to glow in the
city lights, and the wind in the cabin dies. I pour Sheldrake
a cup of tea. "I'm sorry, Lionel. I lost my temper."

"No, it's ... I was out of line." The teacup shakes in his hand. "It's not my place to say. . . . But I do care. And I worry. I feel like you're letting important business slide."

"I'll decide what's important," I tell him. "And as for rigging the votes—I will if I have to. But why bother when it's so easy for me to win?"

Chapter 24:
HOW TO RUN FOR CLASS PRESIDENT

Make posters to put up at school.

That's it.

There are no issues to debate in a student-council election. There are no tax rates to be cut, no bond measures to be passed, no perverted practices to be outlawed. Student councils don't *do* anything. Maybe if you go to a school that has a radio in the cafeteria, the student council will decide what station is played on the radio.

My school does not have a radio in the cafeteria.

Since there's nothing important to talk about, student-council campaigns are massively simple operations. Just poster board after poster board reading VOTE FOR ME! taped up wherever the principal lets you. Our ancestors fought the Revolutionary War so we'd have the right to do this. They must be so proud.

The first posters of the eighth-grade presidential campaign have popped up outside Ms. Sokolov's room. One is made of three strips of red, white, and blue:

I wonder if that might not be too intellectual for my classmates.

My mother's contribution is taped up right next to it. It's a piece of cardboard so heavy with paste and glitter and plastic flowers that it's nearly falling off the wall. It's message: Vote for Watson! He will make the best President!

Or that's what it's *supposed* to read. Someone has crossed out **PRESIDENT** and written **DOODY** in red Magic Marker.[89]

---

89. Handwriting analysis will prove that this was written by Jacob Wong, a sixth grader. He will always wonder why his favorite TV show was suddenly canceled.

I turn away from the posters and find myself facing Tatiana, who has a psychotic smile smeared across her mouth. I try to step around her, but she laughs—a tinkling elfin river of laughter that runs through a shadowy valley of scorn. Shame compels me to turn my back to her. I stare straight into the madness that lives in her dark-brown eyes.

"We got our work cut out for us, don't we, Tubs?"

I nod like a dummy. Tati gives Mom's poster a lazy tug that sends it crashing to the floor. Then she blows me a kiss and skips into Sokolov's room.

Oh yeah. Tati's back. Someone anonymously sent Mr. Pinckney photographs proving Jordie Moscowitz was the graffiti vandal, and Tatiana returned this morning like a triumphant hero. Her mom dropped her off at school in a brand-new pink Mercedes some uncle they'd never heard of left them in his will.

Megan Polanski, the Most Popular Girl in School, watched with undisguised envy as Tati climbed the front steps. "Why are you so lucky?"

Tati didn't miss a beat. "'Cause I'm so good."

Randy Sparks is using the last few seconds before study hall to hand out stickers that read I'M VOTING FOR RANDY.

Most of the people walking by ignore him. Most of the ones who don't ignore him push him out of their way. And most of the ones who don't do *that* take a sticker and then drop it immediately or paste it on the first locker they pass. He'll get in trouble for that.

Verna has to do better. It's important that Randy's campaign not look like a *total* joke, or I run the risk of having Daddy tell me, "It's not a real election, man." "Tell Sheldrake to arrange a sit-down with Verna," I mumble.

"What's that?" says Randy, who I've walked up to.

"Can I have a sticker please, Randy?"

Randy looks confused. "Um . . . Oliver, the stickers say I'M VOTING FOR RANDY."

"Ha-ha!" I say. "That's the same name as you!"

Now he looks *really* confused. "That's because it is me. Look, Oliver, you're my opponent. You really shouldn't—"

"You won't give me a sticker?"

"No..."

"Why are you always picking on me, Randy Sparks!" I bawl. "I want a sticker!"

"Okay! Okay!" Randy's fingers flutter like overcaffeinated butterflies as they peel a sticker off and stick it to my chest. "Pretty," I say, admiring my shirtfront. The bell rings, and I strut into Sokolov's room like a prizewinning peacock. Randy watches me go, baffled. I have that boy so off-balance it's a wonder he can stand upright.

La Sokolova calls the roll like normal. She doesn't pause when she gets to "Lopez, Tatiana." She doesn't even take a few minutes to apologize for "mistakenly" getting Tati kicked out of school. In fact, Sokolov doesn't look sorry at all; if anything, she looks annoyed. Maybe that's because Tati hasn't stopped grinning at her since class began.

I raise my hand. "Can I go to the bathroom?"

Sokolov makes a dismissive hand gesture, like she couldn't care less what I do. So I smile gratefully and walk out the door. But instead of taking a right, to the boys' room, I turn left. There is a small grouping of three lockers located between Sokolov's room and the next classroom down the hall (which belongs to a genuinely insane math teacher named Mr. Rizzo). These lockers look like all the other lockers at school—they even have dented padlocks attached to them—but they aren't assigned to any students. They were installed last year, when the school underwent a major renovation.[90]

I head for the center locker and give its lock a few quick twists. The locker swings open, as do both of the lockers next to it—they're really just one big door. I slip inside and pull it shut behind me.

I'm greeted by an elderly English butler. "Good afternoon, sir."

This is unexpected.

First I squeak—*eeee!*—like a little pig-shaped balloon with a hole in its side. Then I muster an embarrassingly high-pitched, "Who are you?" I'm afraid it's *too* high-pitched, because the butler doesn't seem to have heard me. I could probably only be heard by dogs. Finally, I take a deep breath and manage a slightly lower, more manful, "Who are you? What are you doing here?"

---

90. The job was done for a very reasonable fee by the Sheldrake Construction Company.

189

"I'm Lucan, sir. The butler. It's my job to keep these rooms tidy."

He stands in the dark little anteroom, completely calm and motionless, like a forgotten idol in an abandoned temple. He looks to be about eighty, perfectly attired in topcoat and black bow tie. And, I should emphasize, he seems completely unsurprised to see me. Which is strange, because even though I built this observation chamber over a year ago, this is the first time I've had a reason to visit it.

"Lucan, were you expecting me?"

"Sir," he says, as he pulls out a small brush and starts flicking lint from my shoulders, "I expect someone to walk through that door every day."

"And has anyone ever—"

"You're the first," he says, with absolutely no change of expression.

Now that's a good butler.

"We'll talk later, Lucan," I say, "Right now, I'd like an ice-cold lemonade and a plate of gingersnaps."

"As you wish, sir," he says, and pushes open a heavy oak door into the main chamber. I'm greeted by the bluesy sounds of Captain Beefheart's "So Glad," playing softly over hidden speakers, and Lollipop, who jumps up to lick my face. The room is softly lit and decorated with touches befitting a gentleman's library—fine art, dark-wood paneling, and a two-hundred-year-old Oriental rug. There's a small blaze going in the fireplace, which is unnecessary this time of year but certainly soothing. Lolli curls up next to the fire and is napping instantly.

There's another door at the far end of the room, which I suppose leads to Lucan's living quarters. He disappears through it to mix up my lemonade. Next to it is an eighteenth-century Chippendale cabinet, which hides the entrance to the tunnel my minions used to bring Lollipop here today. In the center of the room is a very comfortable leather chair. And in the middle of the chair is the Electrolyzer.

I pick it up and sit down. "Screens up," I command. Instantly, the walls in front of me and behind me become transparent, allowing me to see into Rizzo and Sokolov's classrooms. I invented two-way dry-erase boards three years ago. They're like two-way mirrors, but with dry-erase...Oh, you can figure this out, can't you? I wasn't sure how to use them at first, but then I realized it might be useful to watch teachers without them watching me.

Rizzo, who is fat and bearded, is playing the ukulele for his pre Algebra class. Like I said, he's insane. I swivel my chair to face Sokolov's room. The class is much as I left it. It's study hall. Some of my classmates do homework; most of them pass notes.

There are some notable exceptions:

QUATTLEBAUM, PAMMY: Has her rhyming dictionary open and appears to be writing another one of her awful poems. She's trying to think, so her fleshy face is twisted up even uglier than usual.

SPARKS, RANDY: Has chewed off the back of his pen and is using notebook paper to mop up a giant ink stain on his shirt.

EXCHANGE STUDENT, MYSTERIOUS CHINESE: Is running a portable electric razor over his cheeks.

LOPEZ, TATIANA: Leans back in her chair to pinch **MICHAELS, LOGAN**, who pretends to be annoyed but actually looks delighted by the attention.

Paying no attention at all is **SOKOLOV, LUCY**, who has her nose buried in another Nabokov novel. She reaches for her silver fountain pen to underline a passage.

I point the Electrolyzer at the pen and squeeze the trigger. Zap.

She drops the pen. Her mouth goes open in a circle; I assume she's saying, "Ow," but I don't have the sound turned on.

Well, we've all gotten little static shocks before. No mystery there. Sokolov reaches for the pen again. I pull the trigger again. Zap.

She drops the pen, her mouth makes a circle.
She tries to pick it up ten times. . . .

Zap. Zap. Zap. Zap. Zap. Zap. Zap. Zap. Zap. Zap.

. . . before she quits.

She's not saying, "Ow," anymore. I'm no lip reader, but she appears to be hissing some extraordinarily foul curse words. The class is looking at her now, wondering what in the world she's up to. Annoyed, she points a finger at them and seems to be saying something about "You mind your own business, you despicable little gutter rats." Her other hand rests on the stapler[91] on her desk.

Zap.

---

91. The Electrolyzer only works on objects that conduct electricity well, like most metals. That's science.

Sokolov jumps up like she's been bit. She's cursing again—and I don't think I've ever seen words like these formed by a human mouth. I'm tempted to turn up the sound so I can learn something new.

"Your cookies and lemonade, sir," says Lucan, offering me my mid-afternoon snack on a silver platter.

"Thank you, Lucan."

The class is now looking at Sokolov with terror, like she's gone insane. And not cute insane, like Rizzo and his ukulele. Dangerous insane, like Lizzie Borden and her axe.

All except for Tati, that delighted, delightful girl, who is laughing, laughing, laughing, and making no attempt to hide it. Sokolov stomps over to Tati's desk, eager to take out her frustration on something or someone she can understand. She's leaning over Tati now, yelling. Tati is doubled over with laughter—oops! By bending over, Tatiana reveals the cell phone hidden in her jacket pocket. Ms. Sokolov smiles wickedly—cell phones are forbidden in classrooms. She plucks the cell phone up, ready to stash it in her desk drawer until the end of the school year.

Zap.

Sokolov drops the phone, nearly hitting Tati, who is rolling on the floor, laughing. Sokolov looks genuinely scared now. And Tati isn't the only one who's laughing. Most of the class is at least smiling by now, all except for that suck-up Pammy Quattlebaum, who looks like she's angry at the world for attacking one of her precious teachers, and Randy Sparks, who just looks confused.

Tati, like a puppy playing a game, picks up her phone and, still lying on her back, hands it up to Ms. Sokolov. Sokolov hesitates, unsure what to do. Then she reaches for it.

Zap.

Lollipop sniffs her nose and whimpers. The room reeks of ozone. "Lucan," I order, "spray some air freshener."

"Right away, sir."

Sokolov has had enough. Enough of these laughing students, enough of this painful room, where everything she touches *bites* her. She makes a beeline for the exit, her face contorted with a mixture of fury and fear.

Did I mention I closed the door on my way out?

Zap.

Twenty minutes later, Sokolov is crouching, her eyes full of hate, her fingers curled into threatening claws as she makes attempt after attempt to turn the doorknob. She looks like a caveman doing battle with a saber-toothed tiger.

Even Randy is smiling now.

I'm enjoying my second helping of cookies. The lemonade, by the way, is pink.

Chapter 25:
TRANSCRIPT FROM A PLEDGE DRIVE[92]

(*Setting: a public television studio*)

(*A man with glasses and a woman whose teeth are too big for her mouth stand in front of a table full of people answering telephones.*)

MAN WITH GLASSES: And welcome back!

WOMAN WHOSE TEETH ARE TOO BIG: We hope you're enjoying our special encore presentation of *The Five Baritones Sing Joan Baez's Greatest Hits*.

M.W.G.: I know I am! It's truly television at its finest.

W.W.T.A.T.B.: That is so true.

M.W.G.: But what I also enjoy this time of year is hearing the sound of phones ringing. Because that means we're getting pledges from you, our viewing audience. Remember, we here at the station can't do our work, which is so vital to the community, without your generous support.

W.W.T.A.T.B.: That is so, so true.

M.W.G.: So give us a call, won't you? Tanya, what gifts are we offering this hour?

---

92. Want to know something funny? I actually don't hate public television. Just the station my Daddy runs.

W.W.T.A.T.B.: Well, with a gift of only forty dollars, you receive this beautiful coffee mug.

M.W.G.: Am I seeing right? Is there a cartoon on that mug?

W.W.T.A.T.B.: There sure is. It's a drawing of the great poet T. S. Eliot, only he's dressed up like Garfield the cat—

M.W.G.: (*fake laugh*) That's funny!

W.W.T.A.T.B.: That is so true! And it'll look just great on the mantelpiece, or on a knickknack shelf, or even to drink coffee out of—

(*A commotion on the set: Phone-answerers put their phones down and start whispering to each other. A few stand on their chairs.*)

W.W.T.A.T.B.: What's going on?

M.W.G.: Sorry, folks, there seems to be some sort of disturbance in the—

(*Sheldrake walks in front of the cameras.*)

SHELDRAKE: Hope I'm not intruding.

M.W.G.: Oh my goodness! Folks, we have a special surprise guest in the studio. It's Omaha's favorite businessman, Lionel Sheldrake!

SHELDRAKE: Please excuse my interrupting like this—

W.W.T.A.T.B.: Don't be silly!

SHELDRAKE: But I was sitting at home, watching your pledge drive, and I thought to myself, "Lionel, you've got to go down there and do something."

M.W.G.: So you're a fan of the station?

SHELDRAKE: No, not at all.

M.W.G.: You're not?

SHELDRAKE: That's what I said. Generally, I'd rather floss my teeth with piano wire than watch public television.

M.W.G.: Erm ...

SHELDRAKE: I mean, I like it when you run Sherlock Holmes mysteries, but I can just download those, right?

M.W.G.: Erm ...

SHELDRAKE: Anyway, it's kind of stupid to pretend that any television show is better for you than any other television show, right? They're all just ways of wasting time. Especially when the supposedly "good" show is something as asinine as *The Five Baritones Swallow Their Own Vomit.*

W.W.T.A.T.B.: That is so true.

M.W.G.: Tanya!

W.W.T.A.T.B.: Sorry ... it was automatic ...

M.W.G.: For your information, the baritones are singing Joan Baez—

SHELDRAKE: Whatever. So, how much were you hoping to make?

M.W.G.: Pardon?

SHELDRAKE: From this pledge-thing extravaganza. How much?

M.W.G.: Well, our goal this year is a million dollars. We'll probably fall a little short, but with the generous help of our viewers at home, many of whom *love* the Five Baritones and the decades of musical experience they represent—

(*Sheldrake rips a check from a checkbook, hands it to Man With Glasses.*)

SHELDRAKE: Here.

M.W.G.: What's this?

SHELDRAKE: A check for two million.

M.W.G.: Two million dollars! Wow! Mr. Sheldrake, that is extraordinary! I guess you really *do* see the value of quality local—

SHELDRAKE: Now shut this crapfest down.

M.W.G.: Excuse me?

SHELDRAKE: I can't stand to see people grovel. And you, sir, are the very worst at it. Nauseating. I'm willing to pay almost anything to shut you up. So here's the money. Now turn off the cameras, send these poor jerks answering the telephones home, and end this.

M.W.G.: End the pledge drive?

SHELDRAKE: That's right.

M.W.G.: But this is our *first night—*

W.W.T.A.T.B.: For God's sake, Oliver, take the money!

M.W.G.: We'd be selling our souls!

W.W.T.A.T.B.: I don't care. I just want to stop looking at stupid coffee mugs and stupid fat baritones and go home and take a long bath.

SHELDRAKE: Do we have a deal?

M.W.G.: Erm . . .

SHELDRAKE: Good. Nice meeting you.

(Sheldrake exits. Woman Whose Teeth Are Too Big For Her Mouth follows him out, as do the people answering the phones. Man With Glasses stares into the camera with a lost look in his eyes.)

M.W.G.: Well, I . . . I guess that ends our annual spring pledge drive. It's funny how things work out sometimes and . . . that's great, so . . . Now, without any further interruption, we return to . . . the Five Baritones. . . . *(long sigh)* Just roll the tape, Charlie. Just roll the freaking tape.

Chapter 26:
A VISIT TO STATELY SHELDRAKE MANOR

"Nice place you got here," says Verna Salisbury, running a finger across Sheldrake's silk couch.

"Thank you," says Sheldrake. "I decorated it myself."

Actually, I decorated it *myself*, and I happen to know Lionel hates it. It's all intricately carved seventeenth-century French antiques and woven wall hangings of knights fighting dragons. Lionel says it looks like the ladies' room at a fancy restaurant, but I think it's important that the home of the fourth-richest man on earth should make a certain *impression*.

"Who's that?" asks Verna, pointing at me. She's pretty, in an intensely intelligent sort of way. All flashing eyes and dark hair and arching eyebrows. A pair of tortoise-shell eyeglasses perches on the end of her long flutelike nose.

"That's my grandfather," says Lionel. "Pay no attention to him. He's in a world of his own."

"Bloogle," I say. My face itches but I won't scratch it; I don't want to tear off any of the wrinkles.

"Saw you on TV the other night," says Verna. "You really destroyed that guy."

"Bloogle!" I scream happily, clapping my hands. "Bloogle!"

"Grandfather, please calm down." He puts a steadying hand on the arm of my wheelchair. He already knows how happy I am with his performance on Daddy's station; this morning, I donated a new building to the Cornell University Medical School in Lionel's name.

"So, Ms. Salisbury," says Sheldrake, putting a this-is-business tone into his voice. "How do you think your assignment is going?"

"Couldn't be better," she says. "I've got the both of 'em— Scott and Randy—wrapped around my little finger. To be honest, after so much time in Washington, I'd forgotten people could be so..."

She hesitates, searching for the right word. "Gullible?" Lionel offers.

She shakes her head. "No. *Sincere*. They're really very sweet."

"So you don't mind . . . your romance with Mr. Sparks."

Verna's lips twist into a lopsided grin. "I'd hardly call it a romance. He gives me a kiss on the cheek after we watch a movie. But no, I don't mind. Like I said, he's sweet."

"Bloogle," I say sternly, commanding Lionel to get to the meat of the conversation.

"Ms. Salisbury, I have some concern that the campaign you're running for Randy Sparks may not be as solid as I'd like. It can't be a joke. It has to look like he has a legitimate chance of winning."

"You want him to lose, right?" says Verna.

"Yes, that's the agreement."

She grins again. "Then you can't ask me to run much of a campaign. I mean, Randy's no natural-born leader of men, but this chump he's up against is a *real* loser. I saw him one time when I was picking up Randy from school. Five foot tall, maybe two hundred pounds. Looks dumb as a post. I hear one time they caught him dunking bologna in a jar of grape jelly—"

"Bloogle!" I shout. "Bloogle!"

"Pipe down, Gramps," says Verna. "Anyway, this kid

Watson, he's just *weird*. When he walks, it looks like an ostrich egg wobbling down the street—"

"Bloogle!"

Sheldrake holds up a hand. "That's enough, Ms. Salisbury. Thank you. Just do me a favor and try to give Randy a slightly more credible campaign. Don't worry about winning. If he starts doing *too* well, I'll just have you sabotage his speech on election day. Agreed?"

"Hey, you keep the checks coming, and I'll do whatever you want," replies Verna, laughing. It's a charming laugh. She could probably run for office herself if she actually cared about anything.

But, like most people, the only thing that interests her is cash. Which makes her very easy to control.

And, for the record, I wasn't dunking my bologna in grape jelly.

It was strawberry jam. I command you to try it some time. Delicious!

Chapter 27:
SUDDENLY, MY HOUSE SMELLS
LIKE LIP GLOSS

Tatiana has turned my family's garage into WATSEN 4 PRESDENT CAMPAN HEADQARTERS. It should, of course, say WATSON FOR PRESIDENT CAMPAIGN HEADQUARTERS, but Tati let Liz Twombley paint the sign that's in the front yard, and Liz learned to spell by text messaging.

Under Tatiana's management, the garage now looks like an evil version of Santa's Workshop. Liz and Logan Michaels are the elves, cranking out poster after poster, dripping paint, paste, and glitter all over the hood of Mom's Buick. Tati is the evil Santa. She sits in a folding chair, leaning back against the wall, leafing through my mother's giant stack of old *Knitter's World* magazines, and yelling at Logan and Liz whenever they take a break for more than two minutes. "Move your keister, Michaels," she barks. "This tub of lard ain't gonna elect himself."

Mom and I watch them through the window while I eat my after-school grilled cheese. The sandwich is gritty; some of Tati's glitter has floated into Mom's kitchen.

My mother has a serious expression on her face as she watches the girls work. After thinking for a long while, she finally says, "Oliver."

And I say, "Yes, Mom"

And she says, "I know all the girls are in love with you. But don't commit yourself too early. You have plenty of time to find the right one."

I nod and promise I'll talk to her before I get married.

Tati pokes her sharp face through the door. "Hey, dork— guess what? We got a spy inside the Sparks campaign."

"What do you—stop it, Lolli!"

Lollipop has jammed her nose up under Tati's sweater and is licking her belly. But Tati is giggling and doesn't seem to mind. "That's okay. I got a dog at home who does the same thing. But listen, Tubby. Somebody keeps texting me the slogans Randy Sparks is gonna have on his posters. Know what that means? We can *respond* to his posters before he even puts 'em up."

"But who would do that?" asks my mother, who's looking at Tatiana suspiciously.

Tati gives her a serious look: "Team Tubby has spies everywhere, Tubby's Mom."

Mom gives a dismissive sniff. She doesn't like Tatiana much anymore. I don't think she minds it that Tati calls me Tubby or Dork or Fat Farm.[93] If I didn't know better, I'd think Mom was jealous. Very strange.

Liz rushes in, squiggling and shaking in her jean shorts and giggling uncontrollably. Her face is marked with big wads of Elmer's glue, like zits. "Can I use your bathroom, Mrs. Watson?" she squeaks. "Logan poured glitter down my underwear, and it itches like crazy."

"Go ahead, dear," says Mom, cold as ice. See? She doesn't even like Liz now, and Liz is *nice*.

"Pretty girlie!" says Liz, patting Lollipop's head as she skips away to the bathroom. I'm starting to think Liz may be smarter than she looks.

"You wanna make a poster, Tubby's Mom?" asks Tati, suddenly polite. "It would be, like, an honor. We got lots of supplies. We stole 'em from Liz's dad's office."

I stare at Tati, astonished. I've never seen her treat an adult with this much respect before.

Mom bites her lip and gives Tati a funny look. "Are you sure you want my help? I thought you girls were taking over."

---

93. That's a new one.

"Oh, no way, Mrs. Tubby's Mom. We totally need your expert advice and everything."

Mom looks like she won the lottery. "Well, if you *need* me, I can't very well say no, can I?" And she tears off her apron and runs out to the garage.

Tatiana watches her go and smiles. She doesn't look so polite anymore. She winks at me and says, "They're like violins. You just gotta know how to play 'em."

Then she walks out the door and slams it in my face.

Is this what love feels like?

Chapter 28:
CALL AND RESPONSE

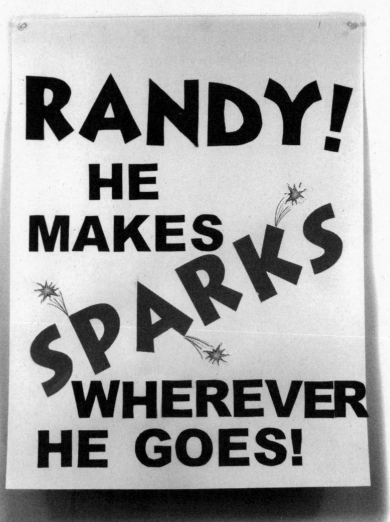

RANDY! HE MAKES SPARKS WHEREVER HE GOES!

WHY SETTLE FOR SPARKS WHEN YOU CAN HAVE LIGHTNING! OLIVER FOR PRESIDENT!!!!

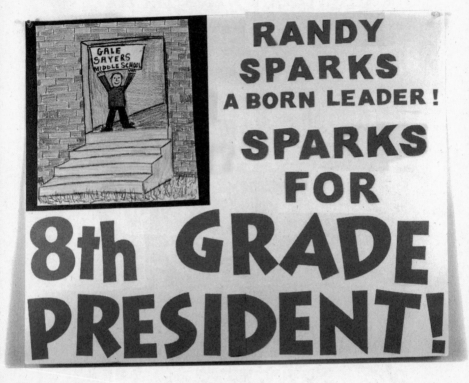

94. Tati made this one herself.

Chapter 29:
EXTREME MAKEOVER—DORK EDITION

Randy Sparks looks good.

I mean, not *good*. He's still Randy Sparks, after all. But Verna has cleaned him up considerably. He combs his hair now. He has new glasses that aren't bent and scratched and taped together. He's washing more often, too; his face no longer looks like it's coated with goat saliva.

His shirts don't have sweat stains around the armpits anymore, but that's only because Verna threw out all his old shirts and bought him new ones in bright preppy colors. I paid for them, of course.

But they're already paying off. Just ten minutes ago, a girl noticed Randy for the very first time in his entire life. I witnessed this momentous occasion. She passed our table in the cafeteria and said, "Nice shirt, Randy." He was so surprised he forgot how to breathe for about three minutes and nearly passed out into his pudding cup.

Now, don't be too impressed. The girl was India Danko, a

very low-ranking female who has one nostril bigger than the other. And everyone hates her because she steals. But she's still definitely a *girl*, which means something. I know it does to Randy; he's been smiling ever since.

With these improvements, Randy is now only the Fifth Most Pathetic Boy at School. The new rankings are[95]:

NAME OF PATHETIC BOY	WHAT MAKES HIM PATHETIC
1. Ted Philips	Cried on first day of school when his mom dropped him off.
2. Benito Guzman	So shy he eats lunch under his desk.
3. Parker Albanese	Doesn't know Mitch Markham makes fun of him behind his back.
4. Mitch Markham	Is best friends with Parker Albanese.
5. Randy Sparks	Is Randy Sparks.

"Randy," I say, as I expertly scrape the cream-filling from my cupcake, "Do you like India?"

He turns pink. "Uh . . . no. I mean, I don't *like* like her." Then he thinks about it and says, "Actually, I don't even regular 'like' her. She stole my jacket last year."

"I think maybe she likes you."

---

95. I, of course, do not appear on the list, since I only *pretend* to be pathetic.

He thinks about that some more. "Yeah," he says, "I don't know . . . but maybe she does."

He tries to take a bite from his tuna-fish sandwich, but it's hard to eat when you're grinning ear to ear.

I'm proud of Randy. He's slowly becoming worthy of getting crushed by me.

Chapter 30:

I WILL BE VERY HONEST. I DID NOT SEE THIS ONE COMING

There is something rotten in the state of Nebraska.

Namely, Alan Pitt's feet, which smell like ass. Har.

But let's be serious for a moment.

Seriously, they smell like butt. Double har!

Sorry, sorry. I'm in a bit of a bubbly mood. Things really seem to be falling into place—and not always in ways I'd expected.

For instance: I've always worried that Mom didn't have enough friends. To be precise, she's never had *any* friends. Not that she isn't friendly. I've watched her try to buddy up with some of the other mothers at PTA meetings and school carnivals. They always act nice enough to her at first, and they always say perfectly friendly things, but then they always, always, always end up ignoring her.

The other moms will stand in a circle, gabbing and laughing with each other, clearly having the time of their lives. Mom stands by herself on the other side of the room, lingering by the snack table, pathetically watching them. It's like they can *smell* something wrong with her. Like wild dogs driving a sick member from the pack.

I've hired actors to be friends with Mom in the past, but she can smell something wrong with *them*, and invariably starts avoiding them because she thinks they're "phony." Mom has a good nose.

Which is why I'm so pleased that Mom finally has friends. Granted, they're twelve-year-old girls, but it's a start.

The day after Tati invited Mom to help make posters, the WATSEN 4 PRESDENT CAMPAN HEADQARTERS moved from the garage into the kitchen. Now, every day as soon as school lets out, Mom sits at the counter with Logan and Liz, giggling in a fog of glitter. Tati sits at the kitchen table painting her nails and ordering them to "stop cackling like morons and get back to work." It's sweet.

But I suspect they're up to something. Yesterday, I went to the fridge for a chilled Twinkie,[96] and they all shut up as soon as I walked in the door. They were all staring at me

---

96. Of course, I have a warehouse full of refrigerated Twinkies downstairs, but somehow they taste better when Mom puts them in the fridge.

and smiling strangely, like I had a booger on my cheek.[97] Liz's stare was especially intense—her eyes were bugging out like she was holding her breath. Suddenly, she burst out, "We have a surprise for you, Ollie!"

Logan gave her a mean kick on the ankle and said, "You're not supposed to say."

Liz looked unrepentant. "I didn't say what it *is*, Logan!"

"Knock it off," said Tati. "Liz—ten push-ups for opening your trap. Logan, you do twenty for kicking her. I'm the one who gives out discipline here."

Logan and Liz immediately dropped to the floor and grunted their way through some very sloppy push-ups.

This was intriguing. I turned to my mother and opened my eyes their widest. "What's my s'prise, Mom? Is it chocolate?"

She smiled and opened her mouth to answer me, but Tati held up a warning finger and said, "You looking to get some exercise, Tubby's Mom?"

Mom closed her mouth.

Then Tatiana stretched her tiny mouth into a crocodile grin

97. I didn't; I checked.

and said, "Don't get yourself excited, Chubbles. We was just talking some campaign business. The only surprise is that our spy at the Sparks campaign stopped texting me what their poster ideas are. So, you know, we gotta work a little harder to get you elected. That's all."

Somehow, I didn't believe that was the actual surprise they were talking about. Still, it *was* surprising to me; Verna's getting lazy. I decided to deduct some money from her next paycheck.

Then Mom shooed me out of the room. When I was half-way down the hallway they started giggling again.

It's simply the most adorable thing ever: My mother has joined a gang.

Chapter 31:
EXTREME MAKEOVER—MEGA-DORK EDITION

Moorhead looks good.

I mean, not *good*—he's still Moorhead, after all—but better, at any rate. He's a little slimmer. His hair's tidier. His teeth aren't quite so yellow; it seems likely he's ventured into the exciting world of toothpastes that whiten as they clean.[98]

The biggest change, though, is in the way he carries himself. There's a little swagger in the old boy's step this morning. A twinkle in his eye. His fat, self-satisfied mouth is even fatter[99] and more self-satisfied than usual.

"Is everyone enjoying *The Outsiders*?" he asks rhetorically, as he parades up the aisle. "I hope so. It's one of my favorites."

I'm surprised to hear this since a) I actually like *The Outsiders* and b) I didn't know we were reading

---

98. As recommended by cigarette #5.

99. Though it may just *seem* fatter because the rest of him is thinner.

The Outsiders. A quick scan of the room proves I'm the only one still holding a copy of *Fahrenheit 451*. It's possible I should pay more attention in class.

I'm not the only one who's scanned the room. Moorhead appears behind me and plucks the book from my hands. "Still finishing Mr. Bradbury's opus, Oliver?" He pivots his head so everyone in class can see his shining face. "Perhaps *someone's* been a little too busy making campaign posters to keep up with the reading."

He waits for the expected laugh to die down before handing *Fahrenheit* back to me. I smile at him gratefully, and say, "I like the part where they burn the books."

That makes his liverlike lip droop a *little*—but just a little—and he's fully regained whatever wind I took out of his sails by the time he gets back to his desk. "Burning books is yesterday's news, Ollie," he drawls, as he rests his hand on an enormous dog-eared copy of *Gravity's Rainbow*. "Today, we're talking about setting your *imagination* on fire!"

It's like he's found new depths of lameness.

What accounts for this new confidence? Did he win the lottery? Has he been hypnotized? Does he draw strength from just being close to a genuine "smart people" book?

The answer is playing over my earbud. It's a conversation recorded half an hour ago, in the Teachers' Lounge.

(*Sound of teachers lounging*)

(*Sound of someone slurping coffee and turning pages in a book*)

SOKOLOV (*approaching, mutters under her breath*): Little jerks … creeps … morons …
MOORHEAD: Hi, Lucy.
SOKOLOV (*annoyed*): Hi …
MOORHEAD: How's it going? I'm just sitting here . . . reading.
SOKOLOV: So I noticed (*then, a gasp of surprise*) . . . Do you like Pynchon?
MOORHEAD: I dunno. I've never pinched.

Let's pause here for a second, shall we?

May I say to you, Mr. Moorhead—telepathically, if by no other means—*Bravo*?

Bravo!

"Do you like Pynchon? "I dunno, I've never pinched"— exactly the sort of so-dumb-it's-smart wordplay you'd find in the works of both Vladimir Nabokov and Thomas

Pynchon. It's the sort of thing that makes me suspect *he's actually reading the book*.

We return now to the conversation already in progress, after the giggling has died down.

SOKOLOV: That's funny.
MOORHEAD: Yeah, I don't know ... it just came to me ... "Pynchon."

(*More giggles*)

MOORHEAD: So . . . cup of coffee?
SOKOLOV: You know what? Why not? But make it decaf.

And that, my friends, explains the smile on Mr. Moorhead's mug.

Has he made it to first base? No. Has he even entered the ballpark? Not on your life. But has he bought a ticket to the game? You betcha.

He floats through the classroom on a cloud of love. It's fascinating—Happy Moorhead is an even worse teacher than Regular Moorhead. He doesn't notice Jack Chapman, who is passing a note to Shirelle Bunting. He doesn't see Pammy Quattlebaum, who is showing off her own enormous copy of *Gravity's Rainbow*, in a pathetic attempt to gain his respect. All he sees is a rosy romance-filled future with a woman he doesn't realize will make him absolutely miserable.

This calls for a celebration. I'll send him a present. "A dozen red cigarettes, wrapped in a bow, all reading WELL DONE, SIR," I mumble, as my stout and balding Romeo struts and preens at the dry-erase board.

They grow up so fast.

Chapter 32:
JUST ANOTHER SCHOOL ASSEMBLY

If you want to grow a cornstalk, you plant it in topsoil.

If you want to grow a rumor, you plant it in a crowd.

Rumors thrive in crowds. All those people jammed together. All those tongues desperate to talk. All those ears desperate to hear. And the only things stopping those tongues from repeating whatever idiotic story the ears hear are a bunch of tiny, tiny brains. And those tiny brains will believe anything.

This is a big crowd. At least, it's as big as a crowd at Gale Sayers Middle School can get. All the children in the sixth, seventh, and eighth grades—even though the eighth graders will be going to high school next year and won't be voting in the elections. And they bused in the fifth graders from the three elementaries that feed into this school, even though they won't be voting, either, just so they can get a taste of how important student government is.

Plus all the teachers of all those students. A lot of the parents for a lot of those students. Reporters. Curiosity seekers. Cops.

So many people that Principal Pinckney has had to hold this assembly in the parking lot, because the auditorium wouldn't contain everyone. And they're all just standing there, like cattle in a holding pen, facing the stage. Newspaper reporters on one side, TV journalists on the other, common folk jammed in the middle. All hemmed in by the dozen or so news vans that are parked around the perimeter with their satellite poles pointed at the sky. All because the great Sheldrake is going to give a speech.

There are three rumors running through the crowd at this moment. One is **RANDY SPARKS SLEEPS NAKED**. This is supposed to creep everyone out by making them think about what Randy Sparks looks like naked. It also makes him sound like some kind of weird hippie who is into nudism and being in touch with his body and gross things like that.[100] Actually, he wears oversize T-shirts and underwear when he sleeps, but he'd have to bring in pictures to prove it to anyone.[101] My instructions were for this rumor to be planted in the back of the crowd. I want to watch the revulsion on peoples' faces as it works its way forward.

100. Personally, I wear flannel pajamas decorated with choo-choo trains, though it's getting harder to find them in my size.

101. My Research Department can provide him with these pictures if he needs them. They have dozens.

The second rumor is **RANDY SPARKS HATES PIZZA**. If anything, this'll creep people out more than the thought of Randy naked. Who doesn't like pizza? Communists? Terrorists? Communist terrorists? Only someone evil, that's for sure. I'm having that rumor planted in the front part of the crowd.

The third rumor making the rounds is **THE FAT KID CAN SET FIRE TO THINGS WITH THE POWER OF HIS MIND**. I actually didn't plant that one—Tatiana did. She came up with the idea of planting a rumor completely on her own (great minds thinking alike and all; she doesn't know anything about my rumors). I'm not quite sure what she's trying to do with this rumor—maybe make people think I'll set them on fire if they don't vote for me? Ah, Tati. You whip through this world like a gold-plated greyhound, leaving fear and anger wherever you go.[102]

I'm onstage at the moment, seated with the other candidates for class office. Me and Randy (his hair plastered down with mousse) and the other rising eighth graders sit to Principal Pinckney's left. He stands at a lectern giving his introduction.

". . . though not a native of our fair city, he has made it famous as a home of industry. . . ."

---

102. Remind me to buy her a present.

The rising seventh graders sit on his right. Standing in the front row are all our parents. Well, not all—Daddy is at home, sulking. He hasn't been the same since the pledge drive. To be honest, I thought canceling the pledge drive would give him a chance to pay more attention to the election. I hadn't reckoned on what an enormous baby he is.

Mom's here, though, with her new BFFs Logan Michaels and Liz Twombley. All three of them are wearing pink TEAM TUBBY T-shirts. Tatiana stands in front of them, wearing a pink silk kimono that mysteriously appeared in her mother's laundry basket yesterday. It has gold and purple dragons embroidered on it, and it has a big stiff collar that juts out on either side of Tati's face like emerald wings. I never dreamed she would actually wear it to school. Somehow she's getting away with it.

Her arms are crossed in front of her body in the billowy sleeves. She has a focused look on her face as she tries to listen to Pinckney's speech, which isn't easy, because Mom and the girls are pinching each other and giggling behind her. Tati raises one of her dainty cocoa-brown hands and snaps her fingers; Mom, Liz, and Logan shut up instantly.

Verna Salisbury is here, too, with her arm very convincingly draped around Scott Sparks's waist. She's really playing this girlfriend act to the hilt. Scott turns to look at her every ten seconds just to make sure she's really there. Verna makes encouraging faces at Randy, who smiles bravely but looks like he wants to pee himself. I'd feel sorry for him, but it's a well-known fact he's a creepy, pizza-hating nudist.

Pammy Quattlebaum and the other suck-ups have also wormed their way into the front row. Everyone, and I mean everyone, is desperate to hear what the great man has to say.

"And so, without further ado ..."

Thunderous applause as Sheldrake emerges from his phalanx of bodyguards. It's curious to watch him from this angle, to see him almost as others see him, as a figure of respect and power. He stands at the lectern in his rumpled tweed sport coat, his corn-silk hair fluttering in the breeze, looking a bit more now like an extremely wise professor than a Captain of Industry.

"There has been a great deal of speculation as to why I would wish to speak at a middle school assembly, to talk about student council elections. I assure you, I have no sinister ulterior motive. ..."

Except to guarantee that your boss will win the election.

"I simply have a deep and abiding faith in the power of representative Democracy, and when I realized that student election season had rolled around again, I asked Mr. Pinckney to let me say a few words to you, the future leaders of this great nation, about the precious gift you are about to exercise for the first time.[103] About the important decision you are about to make . . ."

This is all just a bunch of meaningless bologna he's using to waste time before he gets to the important stuff. This moment. Now. When Sheldrake tells the good people how, quite unexpectedly, he met a young man here at the assembly who possesses all the gifts of leadership and honesty anyone could hope for in a class president.

"Out of the blue, here at this assembly, I met a young man who has all the gifts of leadership and honesty anyone could hope for in a class president."

Sheldrake will admit that this young man's positive attributes might not be obvious to the naked eye, but Sheldrake has a good feeling about him.

"Oh, maybe it's not apparent to the naked eye . . . but let me tell you, I have a good feeling about this young man. . . ."

And though he isn't telling anyone who to vote for, the ris-

---

103. I hear Alan Pitt exercises his precious gift every day before lunch. Har.

ing eighth graders might want to take a good long look at Oliver Watson Junior.

"And far be it from me to tell anyone whom they ought to vote for, but the rising eighth graders among you would be well advised to take a good long look at—"

That's when the bomb goes off.

At least, I think it's a bomb. I'm no expert on these things, but the part of the stage Sheldrake is standing on isn't there anymore. And there is a BOOM that sounds like God's toilet flushing. Then someone is yelling, "Revenge is ours! Revenge is ours!" And everyone starts screaming.

Now it's just general pushing, shoving panic. People are running in different directions, into each other, in circles. Ms. Broadway stands on a chair, screaming her idiot head off about "terrorists" and "space invaders." Vice Principal Hruska tries to bring her back to reality by giving her a light slap on the face. She breaks his nose with her elbow.

The stage is shaking wildly, like a Slinky made of Jell-O. Randy, who's fallen into my lap,[104] whispers, "Jeepers." But the most interesting thing from where I sit is the sight of the newspaper reporters in the crowd not panicking at all. Instead, they drop their notebooks—as if

104. His hair smells like pineapples.

they were expecting this—and pull ugly-looking fighting batons from their jackets; then they rush the stage, looking like nothing so much as a platoon of highly trained mercenaries. They're the ones yelling, "Revenge!"

They should be taking the stage easily—except an opposing platoon emerges from the crowd to fight them. These are the TV journalists and their camera crews, who have, rather mysteriously, pulled out weapons of their own and are now engaging the newspaper guys in battle, right in front of the stage, as everyone else runs for cover.

My mother is frozen in place, her eyes fixed on me, clearly desperate to save her beamish boy. "Marlene!" barks Tati, "Run!" But even Tatiana's considerable charisma can't convince Mom to abandon me and run for cover. Logan and Tati tug on Mom's skirt, to no effect. She won't budge. Then, suddenly and heroically, Liz takes a running start and tackles Mom around the ankles, pushing her to safety behind a fallen section of the stage.[105] Just in time, too, because the wave of battle immediately washes over the spot where they'd been standing.

It seems to be an even fight, until the TV guys' news vans trundle toward the action, lowering their satellite masts as they approach and pointing them at the newspaper reporters. Funny thing—when they're lowered like that, those

---

105. My scientists will immediately start work on breeding a pet unicorn.

satellite masts look kind of like the antiaircraft guns on an Abrams tank....

It all happens so fast. In fact, I see all of this in the five or ten seconds before one, two, three people suddenly throw their bodies on top of me, shielding me from the action. It pays to have a Pistol, Bardolph, and Nym.

Chapter 33:
AFTERMATH

SHELDRAKE ATTACKED!
Deposed African Tyrant Stages Assassination Attempt!
No Word Yet on Financier's Condition

—Headline, *Omaha World-Herald*, Special Edition, May 2

Pistol, Bardolph, and Nym peel themselves off me as soon as the fighting dies down. Just as I suspected, the new librarian and the Chinese exchange student (whose armpit I've just spent a fragrant five minutes inhaling) are two of my protectors.

The third is Pammy Quattlebaum. She gives me an embarrassed shrug and trots back to the parking lot, joining her friends, who are gathered in a circle hugging and crying. They will spend the next two days squealing with leftover terror, and no one will squeal louder or longer than Pammy.

It's strange, but I somehow like Pammy even *less* now that I know she's not just a brown-nosing drama queen, but also some sort of martial arts master. If only because it means she's a lot harder to kill.

(*Setting: Principal's Office. Time: Late Afternoon*)

AGENT SILVERI: What a mess, huh, Joe?
AGENT JABLON: (*grunts*)

(*Sound of door being thrown open*)

PINCKNEY: I will not be ignored!
AGENT SILVERI: Excuse me, sir, but you can't come in here like this. We're conducting a federal criminal investigation—
PINCKNEY: I will not be ignored!
AGENT JABLON: You already said that.
AGENT SILVERI: Shut up, Joe.
PINCKNEY: I am the principal of this school, this is my office, and I demand to know what is going on here.
AGENT SILVERI: Oh. Mr. . . . Pinckney, is it?
PINCKNEY: That's right.
AGENT SILVERI: First of all, sir, I'd like to apologize for commandeering your office. We'll be out of here just as soon as—
PINCKNEY: I don't care about that. What I want to know is why my parking lot looks like a war zone.
AGENT SILVERI: We're still figuring that out ourselves,

sir. But, as far as we can tell—and this goes no farther than [*inaudible*][106]—

PINCKNEY: I understand.

AGENT SILVERI: Well, this dictator of this African country? The guy who got overthrown a few weeks ago? Mb ... Mbeb ... Joe, can you say this guy's name?

AGENT JABLON: (*grunts*)

AGENT SILVERI: Anyway, this dictator guy gets overthrown, and for some reason, he blames Lionel Sheldrake for overthrowing him. And get this: Not only does he think Sheldrake stole his country, but what's got him *really* steamed is he thinks Sheldrake stole his Boba Fett doll. So he hires these mercenaries to dress up like newspaper reporters and ... Are you all right, sir?

PINCKNEY: (*long pause*) I'm fine.

AGENT SILVERI: Because you look like maybe you're having a heart attack.

PINCKNEY: (*long pause*) I always look like that.

AGENT JABLON: You look like you swallowed a hornets' nest.

AGENT SILVERI: Shut up, Joe.

PINCKNEY: I'm sorry. . . . What did you say was stolen? A Booba what doll?

AGENT SILVERI: Boba Fett. Some kind of *Star Wars* toy. Very valuable. Anyway, the new government there in that African country, they figured the old dictator was up to something, so they sent their own soldiers, disguised as TV reporters, to stop whatever he was doing. Good thing they did, too.

---

106. I assume Agent Silveri says, "this room," but I can't be sure because someone (Agent Jablon?) farts directly into the hidden microphone at this moment.

PINCKNEY: You don't think ... There's no particular reason they chose to make the attack at *my* school, is there?

AGENT SILVERI: Looks like it's just a matter of opportunity. Sheldrake doesn't come out in the open like this too often.

AGENT JABLON: You need something in that filing cabinet?

PINCKNEY: No!

AGENT JABLON: Because you keep looking at it.

PINCKNEY: No, I don't!

AGENT JABLON: Okay, whatever.

AGENT SILVERI: Anyway, sir, we should be out of your hair by this time tomorrow. We've pretty much got this wrapped up.

PINCKNEY: Good, good ...

AGENT SILVERI: Agent Jablon and I have to get back to Washington and figure out who stole those Moon rocks from the Smithsonian. We've got one fingerprint, but you wouldn't *believe* who ... Are you sure you're all right?

PINCKNEY: (*long, long pause*) Fine.

AGENT SILVERI: Because you look—

PINCKNEY: I just sweat. Always do. All the time. No big deal. Ask anybody.

AGENT JABLON: Those are nice cuff links. What kind of stones are those?

PINCKNEY: (*long, long, long pause*) Just stones. Just normal stones. Dug up from the earth. I have to go now.

(*Sound of the door rattling*)

AGENT SILVERI: You're trying to open it the wrong way—
PINCKNEY: I know that!

(*Sound of door slamming open, footsteps leaving*)

AGENT JABLON: That guy's too weird to be a good principal.
AGENT SILVERI: Shut up, Joe.

In retrospect, I should have been suspicious of such a massive press turnout for such a minor speech. It's possible Lionel's been right all along; maybe I *am* taking my eye off the ball.

It is a tribute to the competence of the mercenaries who were hired to make the hit that none of my classmates were injured in the attack.[107]

It is a tribute to their *incompetence* that Sheldrake lived. The localized mini-bomb under the lectern, which was supposed to kill him outright, or at least mortally wound him so the troops rushing the stage could finish him off, only succeeded in blowing a hole in the planks beneath him, which he fell through. He suffered a sprained ankle and about a thousand splinters. Physically, he's fine. Mentally, he's another story.

---

107. Aside from multiple bloody noses, skinned knees, and other boo-boos. Jack Chapman broke a finger, but he probably just had it up his nose when somebody hit him.

He hobbles around the cabin of the blimp with manic energy. "I told you. . . . I *told* you. . . ."

"I know."

"How bad is the damage to our network?"

I look at the piece of paper in my hand, though all this information is burnt into my brain. "He only succeeded in bribing a few operatives at the outer fringes. They only know about you, of course, not me. . . ."

"Well, that's a relief!" he hisses, with an ugly dose of sarcasm.

He's right, of course. This is bad. This is very bad. It is the worst attack my Secret Worldwide Empire has ever faced. But I can't allow him to see that I'm worried. He's too fragile to handle that right now.

"When you come to your senses, I think you'll agree that it is, indeed, 'a relief.' All the turncoats have been Phase Foured—"

"I should certainly hope so. What about our friend in Switzerland?"

"He won't be making any more attempts on your life."

"Phase Four?"

I shake my head. "That's too good for him. No, he's going to eat a big dinner and go to sleep early tonight. After a few unnecessary surgical procedures, he'll wake up two weeks from now as 'Lobster Man' in a traveling Mongolian freak show."

Sheldrake snorts with bitter amusement.

"On a more positive note, we're throwing a pizza party for his country's new government. To say, 'Thanks for thwarting the assassination.'"

"Of course," I continue, "this setback complicates the election immensely. Still, I should be able to beat Randy handily. And even if he somehow pulls ahead in the polls—if I keep it close—I can rig the voting machines and no one will be the wiser."

Sheldrake explodes, like an overripe plum in a microwave. "Will you shut up about your precious election!" he splutters. "I was almost killed! Our organization was compromised! Two platoons of soldiers were able to enter Omaha without anyone from surveillance noticing!"

I struggle to keep my voice calm. "I know all that, Lionel. I've already put the entire network on high alert. Double surveillance of the area. Regular jet patrols over our airspace. We won't take any chances until this thing is resolved."

"Until *what's* resolved? Your middle-school *election*? My God—all of this to gain the respect of a man who doesn't seem to even *like* you—"

He stops suddenly, casts a worried glance at Lollipop, who's curled up on a bench. He's upset, so I decide to ignore the meaningless babble spouting from his lips. I give Lolli a subtle hand gesture. Lionel shivers when she leaps down from her perch and lopes over to him, but she only gives him a friendly nuzzle on the hand with her cold, wet nose.

This doesn't soothe him one bit, and he continues to stump around the cabin like Rumpelstiltskin trying to put his foot through the floor. He points a shaky finger at me and says, "There's going to be publicity, you know. Lots of publicity. This is front-page news for the next two weeks."

I'm surprised. He doesn't underestimate me often. "Yes, there's publicity, but it's contained. I've already had our friends in the media shift their attention to Africa—"

"Yes, but—"

"*And* I've arranged for a teenage honor-roll student from Chicago to go missing . . . starting about three hours from now."

"Oh." He stops pacing. "Is she pretty?"

"Very. It'll be a suspected kidnapping. Suspicious vehicles in the area, weird phone calls to the press, all that." Sheldrake knows as well as I do that his attempted murder will swiftly get pushed off the evening news. The public has an insatiable hunger for missing honor-roll students.

"Where is she really?"

"Camping trip with her Scout troop. She forgot to tell her mother about it."

Sheldrake whistles. It's nice that I'm still able to impress him. Suddenly, he looks calmer . . . but also older. More tired. "And how long . . . how long do I have to stay up here on this thing?"

I give him a guarded smile. "That depends on you. Do you still want to have a drink?"

He licks his lips. "God, yes. More than life itself."

"Then I think you need to stay up here a little while longer." I give his arm a squeeze.

He smiles sadly but gratefully. "Thank you, Oliver. I can't tell you how much . . . I mean, it means so much to me, that you actually—"

I give him a frigid glare, and he knows to shut up. Gratitude can sometimes be just as annoying as whininess. He looks down at the floor. He looks beaten. Whipped.

Do me a favor. If you're ever in Mongolia and happen to go to a traveling freak show, don't throw the lobster boy a peanut. I'm still mad at him.

Chapter 34:
I THINK MY FATHER HAS GONE INSANE

"Sic semper tyrannis,"[108] says Daddy, as he flips stations, looking for news about the attack on Sheldrake.

"The noted businessman and philanthropist remains in seclusion after yesterday's attempt on his life, though a spokesman says he is unharmed...."

Daddy snickers into his bowl of Swedish meatballs. "Of course, he's hiding. They get a little scare and guys like that always show their true colors...."

The TV drones on: "Now, we return to our continuing coverage of the disappearance of Ethel Majeski. As you'll recall, the Highland Park, Illinois, teen failed to come home last night after going to the movies with friends—"

"Bah!" barks Daddy, as he hits the off button on the remote. I am, without exaggeration, stunned. It's the

---

108. Latin for "Bullies get what's coming to them." It's what John Wilkes Booth yelled when he shot Lincoln, which makes it a pretty stupid thing for Daddy to throw around.

first time I've ever heard anyone use the word "bah" besides Scrooge in *A Christmas Carol*. And he seems to really mean it, too.

Daddy looks rough. He stopped shaving five days ago. The whiskers around his mouth are stained with gray gravy from the meatballs Mom made us for dinner. His whiskers are also stained with brown gravy from last night's pot roast and yellow gravy from the turkey we had night before last. So I guess he's stopped bathing, too. Mom is a little too preoccupied these days to notice.

We're eating in the living room. Daddy sits in his favorite chair, staring at the still-glowing screen. I sit on the couch with Lolli, hoping he won't talk to me. We've been exiled from the kitchen by Mom and her gang, who now call themselves the Pink Pythons.

They're not even making posters anymore. They just sit at the counter cackling like mynah birds, and clapping their traps shut whenever I walk into the room. When I went in to get my dinner from Mom tonight, they all looked like someone had superglued their mouths closed.

Except for Tati. She was lounging at the kitchen table in a rather skimpy tube top that reads QUEEN PYTHON. I was surprised, because I'd seen her wearing her silk kimono when she came over—then I saw that Logan had the ironing board out and was pressing the wrinkles out of the kimono for her.

"Big day's almost here, eh, Tubs?"

Election Day. "Yeah," I said. "I'm working on my speech."[109]

Mom bolted out of her chair. "Do you need any help, Sugarplum?"

Tatiana gave Mom a tolerant smile. "Don't worry about it, Moggsy. We're giving Sugarplum all the help he needs right here."

That made all four of them—even Mom—giggle like evil villains in a James Bond movie. I was kind of proud of Mom for that.

"Tubby," said Tatiana, "when we get through with you, you're not even going to need to *give* a stupid speech."

"And then you'll live forever!" screamed Liz, throwing her arms around me.

"Knock it off, Bomb Squad," said Tati, not smiling anymore. "He's not a stuffed animal."

---

109. Actually, two Oscar-winning screenwriters are working on my speech.

"But he's so *soft* ..." moaned Liz, reluctantly releasing me.

Bomb Squad is Liz's gang nickname. Tati is Queen Python. Moggsy is what they call Mom—it comes from M.O.G., which stands for Mother of Greatness. Logan's nickname is Silent But Deadly. She isn't very happy about that.

"Tubby," said Tati, "go eat your dinner. The Pink Pythons got some planning to do in here. And don't make yourself crazy writing that speech. We're gonna win the election for you before you even open your mouth."

Those words ring ominously through my brain now as I sit on the couch sucking on Mom's Swedish meatballs. To be honest, I'm a little concerned. What are they up to? It's never even occurred to me to bug my own house before, but it might be time to plant a listening device in the kitchen....

I don't even notice that Daddy is staring at me until he speaks. "That must have been scary. What happened at school yesterday. The attack."

I look over at him and nod gravely. Behind his glasses, his little turtle eyes are bloodshot and bleary.

Daddy gives me a reassuring pat on the shoulder and says, "You have to understand, a man like that Sheldrake. . . ." He says "man" like it's an insult. "A man like that, he reaps what he sows. He reaps what he sows. And sometimes, innocent people like you suffer for it."

"Okay, Daddy," I say, "I believe you. May I please be excused?"

He looks annoyed. "Listen to me, Ollie. This is serious. Your Sheldrakes of the world, they have a lot of money; they think that gives them the right to push other people around. And usually, they get away with it. Because most people can't do anything to stop them. They just don't have any *choice.* . . ."

Daddy spits on the floor—a shocking breach of household protocol. The man is suffering. I know he's been getting a lot of phone calls from managers of other public television stations, all "congratulating" him for being so annoying that he doubled his pledge goal. "But sometimes there's justice," he says. "Sometimes your Sheldrakes tangle with someone who can fight back. Like this African dictator. I bet Lionel Sheldrake rues the day he ever interfered with *that* man."

I gaze at him owlishly. Daddy, for once, has hit upon a topic that interests me. "I bet Lionel Sheldrake rues the day he didn't *kill* that man when he had the chance."

Now he looks at *me* owlishly. "You surprise me sometimes, son," he says, as he puts his forgotten bowl of meatballs on the floor. Lolli lunges for them, and I let her. "You are always the innocent . . . and then sometimes, you're Machiavelli."[110]

Have I been indiscreet? I replay our conversation in my head. I don't think so. It's okay for him to know his baby has teeth.

"Daddy, can I please be excused? I have homework."

He motions for me to leave. I pause in the doorway and turn back to him.

"Daddy," I ask, "are you gonna come hear my speech?"

He rubs his gravy-stained stubble with the back of his hand. "Uh . . . I don't know about that, champ. I . . . It's not that I'm not proud of you . . ."

Of course not.

"It's just . . . I'm kind of a celebrity in town, and I'm really not feeling up to any public appearances these

---

110. A dead Italian who wrote an early self-help book.

days. But we'll have a big dinner when you get home. To celebrate."

"A victory dinner."

"Right," he says. Then he turns the TV back on and starts scanning the channels again for news about Sheldrake.

And to think: *I'm* the evil one.

Chapter 35:
I FEEL LIKE I'VE BITTEN A LIGHTBULB

Is that blood I taste in my mouth? Have shards of glass carved up my tongue?

No, that's rage I taste. Just rage.

Verna Salisbury looks uncomfortable. She should be. She perches on the edge of Sheldrake's sofa, trying to keep up an air of confidence as she speaks slowly into the speakerphone. "I *know* we had deal, but that's over. My mind is made up. I'm sorry...."

Sheldrake's voice hisses reluctantly over the speaker: "No, *I'm* sorry, Verna."

A panel in Sheldrake's bookcase opens, revealing The Motivator. He smiles and takes a few lumbering steps toward Verna, looking like the unholy child of Frankenstein and an albino hammerhead shark. She laughs. "Don't try to intimidate me with your goon. I know you didn't get as rich as you are by killing people over student-council elections."

She's right. Now that she's called his bluff, The Motivator stops in place and sways on his feet, looking confused. He glances at me for instructions.

She notices. "What are you looking at Grampa for?"

Ah, well. I suppose it's time for me to handle this myself. I push the toggle on the arm of my electric wheelchair and roll myself to the center of the room.

"I'll take over from here, Lionel," I say.

"He speaks!" says Verna, in mock amazement.

"Shut up, Ms. Salisbury. I'll deal with you momentarily."

Sheldrake's voice sizzles through the speaker, "Are you sure . . . Grandfather?"

"Positive." Sheldrake's good, but there's only so much he can do circling five hundred feet above us in a blimp. I turn my chair to face Verna. "How much do you want, Ms. Salisbury?"

"This isn't about money—"

I laugh. "Forgive me. You look funny when you're pretending to be noble."

She gives me a piercing look. "You're not Sheldrake's grandfather. That's makeup. Who are you?"

"You may call me the great and mighty Oz."

She nods. She gets it. "The man behind the man. I see. Well, the story is I quit. I don't want any part of your dirty election. You can have all your money back."

"Would you mind telling me why?"

"Did I ask you why you wanted to fix a middle-school election?"

I feel my mouth contorting into an appreciative leer. "Touché, Ms. Salisbury. But you were paid very well for your lack of curiosity. Now you want to break our agreement. That is bad business. I demand an explanation."

She holds her breath for a moment, then swallows. "Okay, that's fair." Her mask of confidence cracks for the first time. She tangles her fingers up on the coffee table in front of her, stares down at them. "The thing is ... I'm in love."

"With Scott Sparks?"

She throws out a defiant chin, as if daring me to laugh again. "That's right."

The room shakes with the sound of a sudden thunderstorm. Verna looks a little rattled by it—which she should, since it isn't actually storming outside. I control the thunder sounds with a button on my wheelchair. It helps set the mood I desire.

"You hardly know the man."

She nods over emphatically and says, "I know. . . . I know. I sound like a fool. Maybe I'm *being* a fool. If I am, I'll find out, and I'll take my lumps like everybody else. I don't care. I can't help the way I feel."

My tummy rumbles with annoyance. "Lucan," I bark. "Bring me a plate of nachos. But use chocolate sauce instead of cheese."

Verna continues as if I hadn't spoken. "He's sweet. He's sincere. He's everything I stopped believing a man could be. They're not . . . they're not like that in Washington. I just can't do it to him. I can't betray him by throwing the election. . . ."

"Why not?" I ask, with real exasperation. "For heaven's sake, why *not*? Love Scott Sparks if you must. That doesn't mean you have to back out of our agreement."

"But it *does*," she says, shaking her head. "I'm not just in love with Scott. It's Randy, too. And the election.

Everything. The late-night strategy sessions, making posters, eating bowls of popcorn while we work on his speech. This is why I got into politics in the first place. This is the stuff I forgot about. One brave kid, daring to step forward and say, 'Hey, I count, too. . . .'"

Lucan enters with my piping-hot nachos (how does he make them so quickly? It's like he can read my mind). Lolli bounds in after him and puts her paws in my lap.

"I've seen that dog before," says Verna, with a thoughtful look on her face. "Hanging around Randy's school ..."

Damn it. She was supposed to stay in the kitchen. "Keep it up, Ms. Salisbury, and I'll let you see her fangs."

Verna smiles. That was stupid of me. I already know empty threats don't work on her.

Maybe not-so-empty threats will be more effective. "You do realize, I can *make* you keep our agreement. By revealing the nature of our bargain to Mr. Sparks."

Behind her, The Motivator smiles. Blackmail is a strategy he is very comfortable with. But Verna keeps smiling, too. All her grit and defiance are suddenly back. Clearly, I've just played the ball straight into her court. "Go ahead and try," she says. "Do you really think he'd believe you? A mysterious billionaire tries to fix a middle-school election? It's a laugh."

Then she looks serious. Her eyes go flat, her mouth becomes a little line. She's suddenly a parody of bull-headed determination. "But even if he did believe you …even if he did tell me to get lost… go ahead, tell him. Because I won't do your dirty work anymore."

My God. She really does love him.

"The Motivator will escort you out."

She looks startled. "That's it?"

"The Motivator will escort you out."

"Okay, well I have a check here paying you back for—"

"Get out! Get out of my sight! Get out!"

Lolli opens her mouth so wide she positively erases her muzzle with the enormity of her teeth. She stalks toward Verna, who rushes out in a confused flurry, the check fluttering to the floor behind her.

Lucan stands there with my platinum platter of nachos as if nothing has happened.

Sheldrake drawls over the speakerphone, "*That* went well."

I rip off my face in disgust. Damn these humans and their idiotic emotions. They're the only things in this world I can't control.

Chapter 36:
OH, THE HUMANITY

Important days don't look like anything special when they start. Invariably, the sun rises and people wake up. Coffee is swilled and eggs are swallowed. Everybody goes about the business of acting like their lives matter and then, no matter how important the events of the day end up being, the sun invariably sets. The sun rose before the soldiers stormed Omaha Beach on D-Day, and the sun set after Archduke Franz Ferdinand was killed. Sunrises and sunsets are real jerks about putting things in perspective.

Today doesn't look like anything special. The sun hangs in the sky like a slice of faded lemon. The school bus grumbles at the corner like a dying yellow elephant. The NewsChannel 5 traffic copter, which always, strangely enough, follows my bus, hovers overhead like a tame black dragon twirling its tail in circles.

But today is special, and Mom has the sappy grin on her face to prove it. She is smothering me in kisses now, mothering me to the very extreme of my endurance. "I'm so proud of you," she says. "You are my specialest,

specialest, very best boy. And we are going to have an extra amazing dinner tonight to celebrate your victory... *Mr. President.*"

Then she gives me about a thousand more kisses. The school bus blows out a big blue fart to show its annoyance.

Today is the day I get elected president. Verna's defection and Sheldrake's aborted endorsement have thrown a few wrenches into my plans, but nothing fatal. I have a speech tucked into my pocket—two pages of pathetic garbage guaranteed to make everyone in the audience pity me enough to vote for me. And if they don't ... well, my speech is good *enough* that people will believe it when I beat Randy by two votes. After I rig the count. I've got every possibility covered.

Mom leans down and whispers in my ear, "And don't forget ... you've got a special surprise coming your way."

Oh, *that.* "But what is it, Mom? Tell me!"

But for the first time in my entire life, Mom stops hugging me before I stop hugging her. She smiles impishly and skips away into the garage. I give Lolli a kiss on the snout and climb on the bus. Tippy the bus driver doesn't even seem to notice I've gotten on, but he closes the door behind me just the same. I make my way back to my seat, enduring the taunts and jeers of my peers, and prepare to meet my destiny.

Let's be honest, I'm nervous. I've undertaken far greater, far riskier endeavors in the past, but nothing I was ever this personally invested in. This isn't about getting a monopoly on pomegranate production in California. This is about *me* getting elected president. And it's been a lot harder than I've liked. But it will be worth it, tonight, when I'm eating that special victory dinner. When my father, who doesn't even have the guts to come see my speech, is forced to propose a toast in my honor. When he has to shake my hand and say, "Congratulations." When he has to acknowledge me as an equal.

That will be sweet.

I settle back in my seat and let the soothing rhythms of Tippy's growling and my schoolmates' screaming and the *thwack-thwack-thwack* of the helicopter lull me into a state of semi-calm. I should try to appreciate this moment. This is an important day, a historic day.

But my calm is broken by a persistent, annoying *beep-beep-beep* coming from a car that's following us. I try to ignore it, but Stephen Turnipseed says, "Hey, Lardo! Your mommy wants you." I try to ignore that, too, but he says it again and points out the bus's back window. I turn around and look. Sure enough, Mom is following the bus in her Buick, leaning on the horn for all she's worth and waving. Liz and Tati are squeezed into the front seat next to her, with Logan poking her head through from the back.

PINK PYTHONS is scrawled in bright paint across the hood of the car, next to a drawing of the ugliest, most genetically defective, cross-eyed, drooling[111] snake you've ever seen. TEAM TUBBY is written in shaving cream on the windshield. Dozens of balloons and streamers and tin cans are tied to the bumper and the roof rack. They drag like dead kites behind the car.

All of them—Bomb Squad, Silent But Deadly, Moggsy, even Queen Python herself—are smiling the biggest, craziest, toothiest smiles possible. Any psychiatrist who saw them at this moment would quickly throw them into a dark basement for the good of society.

This is their surprise? *This* is going to win me the election? Four hyperactive females in a vandalized midsize sedan? That's not going to win me a game of checkers.

Frankly, I'm disappointed. Not in Liz or even Mom— this is just the sort of affectionate but futile gesture they specialize in. But Tatiana's better than this. She thinks *bigger* than this.

---

111. Maybe the drool is supposed to be venom?

Or so I thought. Ah, well. It was nice of them to try, anyway. I wave back at them weakly and return to my seat.

I decide to distract myself from worrying about my speech[112] by playing with Moorhead a little. He's made steady progress worming his way into Sokolov's affections, following my directives to TELL HER YOU LIKE ITALIAN OPERA and TELL HER YOU LIKE BUSTER KEATON MOVIES. My Research Department tells me Sokolov doesn't know anything about Italian opera or silent movies, so Moorhead can talk his fool head off about them without fear of embarrassing himself. The man is blissful with his success so far. The arrogant smirk on his face these days is probably the same one a male black widow spider wears when he steps onto his girlfriend's web.

It's time to take his courtship up a notch. I will increase the strength of the verb he uses, plus I'll make the remark more personal. Today he will TELL HER YOU LOVE HER TASTE IN MODERN LITERATURE. This is both complimentary and condescending; it's sure to intrigue her. Which means that tomorrow, he'll finally be able to ASK HER OUT TO DINNER.

"Cigarette message for Moorhead," I mumble, to whatever minion is listening. "TELL HER YOU LOVE HER—"

That's when the riot starts.[113]

---

112. Even though I *know* I have no reason to worry.

113. These interruptions are getting annoying.

There is screaming, and jumping up and down on seats, and foot stomping, and window slapping. What's worse, all of it is gleeful. My busmates are positively beside themselves with joy. Perry Wengrow and Stephen Turnipseed push in next to me to get a better view out the window.

A flatbed truck, with TWOMBLEY AMUSEMENTS painted on it, is approaching us from around the corner as we reach Harney Street. But the truck itself is not what's riot-worthy. It's what the truck is *towing*.

An enormous, inflated, hot-air balloon. Maybe forty feet tall. Fully worthy of being floated down Broadway during the Macy's Thanksgiving Day Parade, alongside Snoopy and Mighty Mouse and all the other cartoon dirigibles.

And it's in the shape of Oliver Watson Jr. (*see plate 16*).

Two thoughts immediately rush through my head:
- That balloon makes me look fat.
- My God, *what have they done?*

A quick glance back at my mother's car confirms my fears. Liz and Logan and Mom are bouncing in their seats like Mexican jumping beans with severe attention deficit disorder. This is their *big surprise*. Liz has gotten her father, the inflatable-gorilla king, to make a giant balloon of *me*. One that is *much fatter* than I have

PLATE 16: An enormous, inflated, hot-air balloon.
Maybe forty feet tall. Fully worthy of being floated down
Broadway during the Macy's Thanksgiving Day Parade.

ever been. And now this *monstrosity*—this *abomination*, this *embarrassment*—is going to follow my bus all the way to school.

Tatiana, my sweet. Forgive me. I underestimated you.

She sits in the center of the Buick's front seat, the only one in the car not screaming like a spasmodic banshee. She is calm. Placid. The eye of the storm. Her face is wreathed in a smile so sinister and satisfied that she looks like she just swallowed Big Bird.

She winks at me.

And that's when the *really* bad news hits me.

My network is in a state of *High Alert. Code Red. Triple Security*. All my operatives are under strict orders to *react with extreme prejudice*. Any anomaly is to be treated as a threat until it's proved otherwise.

The balloon is only fifty yards away now, coming closer....

And the whole world goes into slow motion.

Forty-five . . .

"No," I whisper.

Around me, my classmates wave and scream and hop like savages dancing to please their god of destruction.

It's forty yards from the bus now ... thirty-five. ...

"No ..."

Its enormous left foot bounces against the side of a truck, then snags on a small tree and rips it from the ground.

"No," I order. "Don't fire. Stand *down*."

Thirty ... twenty-five ...

Stephen Turnipseed is pounding me on the back and laughing. Big drops of spittle spray from his mouth and splatter across my cheeks, my nose, my eyes.

"Don't fire. ... Please ..."

It runs into an overhead power line and snaps it.

Twenty ...

The broken power cables writhe like snakes with rabies, sending electrical sparks arcing high into the air.

"*Listen* to me!"

Fifteen ...

"No!" I scream, not caring who hears me. "No! Don't fire! Stand down! *Stand down!*"

Maybe the pilot can't hear me over the din of the shrieking animals around me. Maybe he can't understand what I'm saying. Maybe he can hear me, but he's too freaked out by the approaching floating colossus to pay any attention to my words.

Ten ...

All I know is I'm still screaming, "Stand down! Stand down!" when the NewsChannel 5 traffic copter fires an AIM-92 stinger missile right at the heart of the Oliver Watson balloon.

Chapter 37:
REVENGE OF AFTERMATH!

Mom is crying in the school parking lot. Liz and Logan are next to her, hugging each other and whimpering. They'd be crying, too, but I think they're all out of tears by now.

Again, only Tati is calm. She sits serenely on the hood of Mom's car, snickering to herself. She catches me watching her and winks at me again.

No one on the bus can believe they actually saw a lightning bolt strike the balloon out of a clear blue sky. Especially because no one actually saw that. But that's the story I'm having my operatives spread, and since it's the only plausible explanation, the police are buying it.

"Just a giant lightning flash, right out of nowhere," says the pilot of the NewsChannel 5 traffic copter.

"Big flash of electricity," says Tippy the bus driver, who I suddenly realize looks a lot like that nephew The Motivator asked me to give a job to two years ago.

"It was scary! A huge, jagged thunderbolt! I saw the whole thing," says Pammy Quattlebaum, who was five miles away when it happened.

Such is the power of persuasion that even the people who saw the missile—who *know* they saw a missile—are starting to believe they saw lightning strike.

"Biggest bolt of lightning I ever saw," says Stephen Turnipseed. And he gets into a fight with Cory Carter when Cory says he saw a rocket.[114]

Everyone is being very sympathetic toward me. Especially Agents Jablon and Silveri, who were at the airport about to head back to Washington when news of the balloon downing broke. They appear to believe the cover story, but with such a strange incident coming right on the heels of the Sheldrake assault, they decide to stay in town for a few more days.

"A ginormous spaghetti of light came out of the sky!" I tell the agents.

"You already said that," says Agent Jablon.

"Shut up, Joe," says Agent Silveri.

Principal Pinckney nearly fainted when he saw them

---

114. Cory ends up with two black eyes and a belief that he, too, saw a lightning bolt.

drive up. Which is probably why he decided to hold today's student council elections as planned, in the interest of saying, "Nothing to look at here. Just business as usual. No reason for the FBI to hang around this school."

I would tell him how suspicious that looks, but I don't want him to have a stroke.

I lick my palms and smear some saliva under my eyes so Mom will think I've been crying, too. Perversely, that seems to cheer her up a little. It's important to her that I care about the balloon.

"Oh, Ollie," she moans, as she crushes me to her bosom. "It was our big surprise! We worked *so hard!*"

"It was supposed to win you the stupid election," says Liz, who is kicking the tires of Mom's car. I've never seen Liz look this sad before. I didn't know she was capable of emotion this deep.

"I'll still win," I say, and Liz smiles a little. Maybe I won't die after all.

"But that was such a funny lightning bolt," says Mom. "I never saw a lightning bolt that was black before."

"With fins," says Logan.

"Yeah," says Tati. "That was one *craaaazy* lightning bolt." She holds her sides to keep from breaking a rib while she laughs.

She was the one who worried me, in the aftermath. I didn't know what she would say to the FBI when they interviewed her. She was certainly close enough to know it wasn't a lightning bolt that ruined my surprise, and, unlike the others, she's too hardheaded to be convinced otherwise.

I shouldn't have worried. I'd forgotten about her compulsive hatred for authority figures.

Agent Silveri said to her, "Tell me what you saw, little girl."

And she said, "Go climb a tree, G-Man."

So then he said, "What's your name?"

And she said, "Your mother."

He gave up after that. I suspect she does know it was a missile. And I suspect she doesn't care. I think she *likes* a world that's dark and dangerous and doesn't make any sense. It's like she was raised by vampires.

Right now Mom is shooting Tati a dirty look. "How can

you be laughing? We worked so hard, and now it's all for nothing!"

Time for Tubby to save the day.

I push myself away from Mom so she can see the rapturous smile I've constructed on my face. I want her to know I'm happy. "It was the bestest fireworks I ever saw," I exclaim. "Better than the Fourth of July!"

And now "Mom" is happy, too, and hugging me again. "Oh, Sugarplum," she says. "You make everything beautiful!"

"You tell 'em, Sugarplump!" shouts Tati.

"You're the best Sugarplum ever," says Liz, who is suddenly hugging me, too, from behind. Now Logan has squeezed in to hug me, too—tough to do for such a large girl. Somehow they're all crying again.

If I ever manage to breathe, I just might get a chance to give my speech.

Chapter 38:
THE MOMENT YOU'VE ALL BEEN WAITING FOR

And here we are. A school auditorium, throbbing with the voices of a thousand students saving each other seats, tripping over each other's feet, sharing pieces of bubble gum they keep expertly hidden from the eyes of teachers.

And here I am, sitting onstage next to Randy Sparks (again), who's wearing a new blue blazer that actually looks kind of sharp. He's smiling like he's relaxed—Verna must've taught him that—but I notice he has to hold his knees together to keep them from knocking. He turns to me and whispers, "I'm nervous, Ollie."

"Please don't hit me, Randy," I reply. "Not in front of everybody. Do it when we're alone. It's too embarrassing."

I figure it can't hurt to confuse him one last time, just before he speaks.

But it doesn't work. He opens his mouth to protest, then shuts it. He nods, almost wisely. It's like he's learning something about me (or himself) while I watch him. He turns away from me and studies his speech.

There's Tatiana, in the fifth row, writing dirty words on Logan's arm.

There's Megan Polanski, the ex–Most Popular Girl in School, staring daggers at her ex–best friends Shiri O'Doul and Rashida Grant, who are busy ignoring her. They decided yesterday that she "wasn't cool." Rashida's the new Most Popular Girl in School. We'll see how long she lasts.

There's Josh Marcil, his fleshy freckled fingers smeared with chocolate, telling anyone who'll listen that he found a toilet that's full of malted milk balls. He must've crawled through the gap under the door.

There's Jack Chapman, a few seats over, who should, by all rights, be sitting up here in my place. No matter who gets elected today, he'll always be Jack Chapman. If anything, he's become more impressive and all-American since he pulled out of the race. His shoulders seem wider, his eyes seem clearer—he seems to have grown up overnight. The only weird thing is the handkerchief he carries these days, and the way he's always blowing his nose. Well, every great man has his eccentricities.

There's Alan Pitt, whose acne had been clearing up until he called me "Sir Eats-a-Lot" three days ago.[115] Now he scratches miserably at his face, which looks like he's been making out with a slice of pizza.

I don't see Mom, though I know she's here, somewhere, to witness my moment of triumph. But there's Moorhead, patting the seat next to him, which he's saved for *La Sokolova*. She smiles at him from the aisle and pushes her way past Lanny Monkson (who is legally blind) to get to the proffered seat.

Agents Jablon and Silveri stand in the back of the room, glowering importantly. A few feet from me, Mr. Pinckney sweats at the podium, looking like he picked the wrong time to take an extra-strength laxative. "Thank you all for coming," he says, "to what I think is the most important day on the school calendar...."

I tune him out by turning up the sound on my earbud. It's playing my new favorite song, Captain Beefheart's "Yellow Brick Road." I am wearing my favorite jeans and my lucky striped shirt, the shirt I wore when I fixed the Kentucky Derby.[116]

And so the speeches begin. The rising seventh graders start, from lowest offices to highest. Those ambitious

---

115. His conversion to "not being bad" seems to be wearing off. He may need another playdate with me.

116. I like betting on long shots, but I'm not a fool.

souls who want desperately to be seventh-grade treasurer (even though the seventh grade has no money) stutter out their nervous little paragraphs and scurry back to their chairs. The audience pretends to be interested at first, but they soon look like they all wish they had earbuds of their own.

Sheldrake's voice interrupts the song. "Sorry to intrude like this, Oliver, but I wanted to wish you good luck. Though I'm sure you don't need any. I know this is important to you, and even if I don't quite understand why, I'm glad you're getting what you want."

"I also want to tell you how grateful I am." I scowl impotently—he knows I can't tell him to shut up. "I'm almost ready to come down now, and I really want to thank you for giving me this opportunity to get my head together."

Get my head together—that's Daddy language. I'll have to give Lionel a stern talking-to when he lands. There will be no hippie talk in my organization.

"Anyway, break a leg and all that. I'm rooting for you from up here." And the Captain resumes playing.

The rising seventh graders finish their turn, and Penny Trimble is at the lectern now, giving her pitch for why she should be eighth-grade class secretary. I tune down the earbud to hear what she's saying. "...and, if elected, I promise to put pop[117] in the water fountains...." She laughs lamely. The audience laughs not at all, which leads me to suspect she's not the first person to make that particular ancient joke today.

I'm laughing, but only because I'm polite.

I'm distracted by a rustling in the audience. Ms. Sokolov is out of her seat and desperately forcing her way out to the aisle, not even bothering to whisper "excuse me" as she pushes past Lanny Monkson (whose glasses are sent flying). Moorhead watches her go, cheeks flushed, mouth agape, eyes wide with terror. His face could be the international sign language symbol for "What did I say?"

What did he say? And then I remember that my last message to him had been rather rudely interrupted: TELL HER YOU LOVE HER—

I didn't get to finish that one. I was distracted by the giant balloon, and the missile, and the huge ball of fire, and the humanity, and I forgot to correct the dictation. Well. That must have been a pretty freaky thing to hear in a crowded school assembly. He must have sounded like a stalker. I guess that's one budding romance thwarted. Which is too bad, because I thought Sokolov had a real shot at ruining Moorhead's life.

---

117. That's what we call soft drinks here in Omaha.

Actually, by the look on his face now, I suspect she might have done it anyway. My lucky shirt strikes again!

Dylan Berger (a boy) makes his speech for eighth-grade vice president, and Dylan Krakowski (a girl) makes hers. And suddenly, it's time for the main event.

"The office of eighth-grade president is the highest elected position we have here at Gale Sayers Middle School," opines Pinckney, "and the two boys you see in front of you have waged a spirited campaign." His eyes shift nervously for a second over to the Federal Agents standing in the back. "And neither of them have broken any laws ... that I know of. So, you know, it's really just a normal student-council election. Except for the mercenary battle in the parking lot, and that really didn't have anything to do with anyone here. I mean, what connection could there possibly be?" He laughs nervously, then seems to realize it was perhaps unwise for him to stray from his written remarks. "Uh, anyway, they'll be speaking in alphabetical order. Up first, Randy Sparks."

Tepid applause from the crowd. Randy's legs don't work for a second; then he grits his teeth and wills himself out of his seat. He walks—not confidently, but purposefully, like he has to consciously think his way through every step—to the lectern. He opens his mouth. Nothing comes out. His lips curl into a simpleminded grin.

Someone stage-whispers, "Go ahead," from the audience, and then I see Verna, beaming at Randy from ten rows back, with a smile of pure faith on her face. Scott Sparks sits next to her, holding her hand, and he gives his son a thumbs-up.

It does the trick. Randy's smile takes on the semblance of some intelligence. He begins: "I was eating a big sausage pizza at La Casa last night, talking to my dad about how it was time for me to buy a new pair of pajamas..."

Verna is good. Without even completing a sentence, Randy has just negated both of the rumors I started about him.

"...when Dad reminded me of something my uncle Dave, the fireman, said last Thanksgiving."

Verna is *very* good. The weaker-minded of my classmates will believe that Uncle Dave can protect them from my fire-setting powers.

"Uncle Dave said that the most important thing he'd learned in life is that none of us is perfect, but that we should all strive to be the best person we can be." He pauses self-consciously and glances down at the note cards in front of him. "I know I'm not perfect. ..." he says, then he pauses and smiles, letting the audience know it's all right to laugh. They do. "I know I'm not the most popular guy at school.

I've eaten so many lunches alone I've forgotten how to talk and chew food at the same time."

He smiles again. The monkeys howl with laughter. It's not that good a joke, but it's charming. And it's disarmed Randy's greatest weakness—the fact that he used to be the Most Pathetic Boy in School. It's not a liability if he can laugh about it.

Randy looks down at his notes and stops smiling. Verna has undoubtedly written *look serious* at this point in the speech. He makes a dignified face for the audience. "But this isn't a popularity contest. It's an election. And that means that even a guy like me has a chance."

"I know sometimes it feels like we're just kids, and we never get to do anything important. Well, what we're doing today is important. We're voting. We're picking the people we want to lead us for the next year. And it's not a joke. Our ancestors fought and died for the right to vote. That's not a joke, either. Voting is what makes this country great. We were the first nation to say that all our citizens should get a say in how the government is run. Not a king. Not just some aristocrats or rich people. All of us. And when we vote, we're saying, 'Hey! What I think matters, too!' When we vote, *we make ourselves important.*"

He looks like he believes it.

A quick glance at the crowd. The morons are eating it up.

This is dangerous. Belief is more contagious than chicken pox.

"We're told that voting is a gift. That's true. But it's not just a gift that's given to us. It's a gift *we* give to our government. It's our way of giving the government the benefit of our knowledge, of everything we've learned about the way things ought to be. It's our way of showing we *care* about what happens to our school, our country, our world.

"When our parents vote, they're not just saying, 'I think this or that person should be president.' They're saying, '*I love America.*'

"And when we vote today, we're not just saying, 'I think Randy Sparks or whoever should be on student council.' We're saying, '*I love Gale Sayers Middle School.*'"

Applause. Deafening, resounding, sickening applause. It seems like everyone in the room is clapping except for Verna, who has her hands clasped to her breast and stares at Randy with shining, adoration-filled eyes.

Randy stares down at his cards long enough for the applause to die. Verna must have drilled this into him: "Give them time to settle. Let them hear your final words."

Randy looks up as the last scattered claps come to rest around the room. "I could tell you I don't care who you vote for, just as long as you vote. But that would be a lie. I want to be your class president. But whether you vote for me or my distinguished opponent"—a few unkind titters tinkle their way through the crowd—"I want you to know this: If elected, I will fight for you. For every single one of you. I will fight every day to make this school a better place. For all of us. That's the *duty* of an elected official. And that's my duty. By standing on this stage, I am starting the holiest journey of my life. The journey of democracy. And maybe I'm not the most popular kid in school, but I'll tell you this…"

Pause. Wait for it… wait for it…

"I love Gale Sayers Middle School!"

Applause. Ugly, resounding, redounding applause. Applause that bounces off the rafters, bangs against the walls, pounds against the stage like a wave. Applause and whistles and cheers and screams. The crowd is on its feet. On its feet! As Randy nods humbly and walks back to his seat, as he pauses for a hearty, heartfelt handshake from Mr. Pinckney. *The crowd is on its feet*! Cheering and stamping and clapping.

And there, amid the storm of that standing ovation, I finally see her. My poor mother, sitting in a dark black corner of the auditorium, looking confused and alone and dispirited. She's the only one who isn't cheering, bless her heart.

And my eyes slide over to Mom's right. And I see somebody who isn't supposed to be here.

Somebody who'd said he "wasn't up to" coming to hear
his son speak.

Somebody who is standing and clapping and stamping harder, louder, *faster* than anyone else in the room.
Somebody whose face is alight with joy—who believes—
who actually *believes*—every single insipid half-assed
platitude that just came out of Randy Sparks's weak
little mouth.

Somebody who loves democracy. Somebody who believes
in student government. Somebody who's cheering for
Randy.

And something inside me snaps.

Chapter 39:
MADNESS

There's a buzzing in my ears.

It drowns out everything around me. I can't hear Mr. Pinckney asking the crowd to resume their seats. I don't hear him introducing me. But I see him nod in my direction and walk back to his chair. And I can feel the eyes of the whole room on me.

I am standing at the lectern. I don't remember getting up or walking to it. I'm just here, suddenly, with this buzzing in my ears and all the eyes of the world on me.

I take out my speech. It is a heart-rending document of idiotic catchphrases, foolish thoughts, and appeals to sentiment. It was designed to make these people feel sorry for me.

I rip it in half. The pieces float to the floor like dying birds.

"Fellow students," I say. "Honored teachers. Distinguished guests."

I can't hear my voice over the buzzing.

"We have heard today about the beauty of the democratic process. About the 'gift' we both receive and bestow. My esteemed opponent . . ." Here I bow rather grandly in Randy's direction. He looks at me strangely, like a confused animal. "I say, my esteemed opponent has promised to fight for each and every one of you if elected."

I cock an eyebrow.

"Ladies and Gentlemen," I say. "Students and Teachers. Children of all ages. I put it to you: *What will he fight for?*"

Now I have an audience full of confused animals looking at me.

"Yes, the sentiment sounds pretty. But there's precious little fighting to be done around here, isn't there? Any important decisions about the school are made by Mr. Pinckney and his able staff. I'll go further: Any *unimportant* decisions about the school are also made by Mr. Pinckney and his friends. The truth is, the student government of this school—the student government of *any* school—doesn't really do anything.

"Maybe next year's council will decide to hold a bake

sale. Maybe they'll *decide* which charity they should give the proceeds of that bake sale to. Maybe they'll *decide* what the color scheme should be for the eighth-grade formal."

I raise my hands in mock wonder. "Huge decisions! Gargantuan choices! The sort of judgments mere mortals shrink from making! But the brave children of the student council have sworn to fight, have sworn to make exactly these hard decisions—so decide they must."

I let my breath out in a long, audible hiss, like a pool toy deflating. "Unless, of course, Mr. Pinckney *decides* that they shouldn't hold a bake sale. Or he *decides* they should give the money to an old folks' home instead of the dog pound. Or he *decides* that green and black will better suit the formal than red and blue.

"In the end, what does all that fighting, what does all that *deciding* add up to?" I pause. I let my question sink in. "Pretty words on an empty stage."

The buzzing is louder now. I thought talking would make it quiet down, but I was wrong.

"Student government is meaningless," I proclaim sadly. "Worse, it is *empty*. Null. Void. My distinguished opponent"—I throw another grand bow Randy's way—"says that this is not a popularity contest. But he speaks an untruth. I would not call him a liar. Let us say, he is misinformed.

"If there are no issues to *decide*, no battles to *fight*, what else can this be but a popularity contest? What else can you, the voter, do but pick the one of us you like best?

"That, my learned friends, is the very definition of a *popularity contest*."

I put a melodramatic hand to my troubled brow. "Ladies and Gentlemen. *Messieurs* and *Madames*. *Niños, niñas*, and assorted *bambini*. Allow me, if you will, to veer off course for a moment.

"I spoke before of an emptiness. I said, if you'll recall, that student government was empty. I'd like now, if you'll permit me, to speak of a greater emptiness. This is the emptiness of real government. This is the emptiness of democracy itself.

"Every election year, we're treated to the spectacle of politicians pandering for our votes, pretending they like us so we'll like them. Every year, the pundits bemoan the fact that the issues are getting ignored, that rhetoric is triumphing over facts, that charisma is trumping truth. They complain, in short, that our elections are a popularity contest."

The buzzing is in my eyes now, too. My retinas vibrate in time with the sound in my ears. The faces in front of me shake and blur. It's like I'm looking at the world through the beating of dragonfly wings.

"My friends, my friends, my friends ... what else *can* those elections be, when the very *first* elections most Americans experience, the ones that *teach* us what elections are—and I speak of student-council elections like this one—are quite literally *popularity contests.*"

I shrug. "They beat it into us when we're young. And we never forget it.

"Now, my comrades, my droogies, my pals, you are probably thinking that I'm advocating some sort of reform. I'm leading you up to some place where I'll say, '*We must make these elections matter!*' and, '*We should be casting our votes based on issues, not personality!*'"

I give the fools my warmest smile. "I am saying nothing of the sort. Because the truth is I *want* you to waste your time picking between popinjays.

Now I frown at them, like a family doctor giving an unpleasant diagnosis. "The truth is all these posing politicians and empty issues—they're just distractions. A few baubles to keep you busy while you live and breathe and squirm. Because the real truth is a magic trick. Somehow, magically, all of you, even the poorest, are born clutching a dollar bill in your grubby little paws. Even the starving children on the Amazon basin, even the forgotten babies of Appalachia—they're born holding that dollar. And it's the life's work of people like me to steal or trick or sweet talk those bucks from your grasp.

"And if you're too busy worrying about which candidate is cuter to notice what we're doing, well, so much the better."

I give them the smile of a saint. I feel suddenly clean. So much poison leached from my soul in one geyser of vomit. The buzzing in my ears dies. My eyes stop vibrating. They focus.

And I see a crowd of stunned and angry animals. I see confusion. I see curiosity.

And on Tatiana's face, I see delight. She's a giggling, clapping, joyous nymph.

But "Daddy" isn't clapping. I mean, *of course*, he isn't clapping. But he doesn't look sad, either. Just ... *worried*.

And "Mom" looks like I've punched her in the stomach.

This is wrong.

In one self-indulgent rant, I've ruined myself. With five minutes of truth, I've destroyed a dozen years of lies. I am exposed. Naked. Weak.

My brain races. There must be some way to save the situation. Some way to reassert my idiocy. Some way to reclaim my cover.

And because I am a genius, I come up with the only solution possible.

I step slowly to the front of the stage.

And I pee my pants.

Chapter 40:
(SEE PLATE 17)

PLATE 17

Chapter 41:
GO AWAY

Chapter 42:
SERIOUSLY, GO AWAY

Chapter 43:
FINE

I am walking home. I am walking home and no one can stop me.

I am in a pair of green shorts I stole from the gym. They are too small, and I can feel the elastic cutting an ugly red welt around my waist.

"Burn it," I say. "Burn it to the ground."

In retrospect, peeing my pants in front of the entire school doesn't seem like such a good idea. Yes, it was the only thing I could have done, but is anything, even an empire, worth that kind of humiliation?

Mom's dumb confusion.

 The shame on my father's face.

Tatiana laughing. Laughing harder than I'd ever seen any-one laugh, till tears ran down her lovely face. Tears of joy. My campaign manager, my pink and golden empress laughing, laughing, laughing at me.

Somewhere in this whole mess, I'd forgotten that she's the Meanest Girl in School.

"Strafe it," I say. "Raze it. Reduce it to a pile of ashes." I'm giving orders to my squadron of jets. I'm sending them to my school. I will erase my shame. I will burn it from the Earth. "Destroy it. I want rubble piled upon rubble."

My airbase is in Grand Island, but that's only a five-minute flight at their speed.

"Don't leave a single stone standing."

No one tried to stop me when I ran out of the auditorium. No one wanted to touch me. I left my favorite jeans on the floor of the locker room and slipped into these sweaty green shorts. I ran out the back and passed Mr. Moorhead in the parking lot. He didn't even notice me. He was sitting in his car, tearing open a carton of cigarettes, examining every single one for a message that wasn't there. That would never be there.

"Destroy the walls, then salt the earth. So nothing will ever grow there again."

I hear the distant hum of a squadron of jets roaring in from behind me.

"Rake it. Raze it. Burn it."

"Hey, champ." There's a hand on my shoulder. I look up and see it's attached to my father, who's red-faced and out of breath. "Thought I might find you walking this way." He looks at me and says, "Oh, hey. You're . . . Here, let me clean you up a little bit." He pulls a Kleenex from his pocket and wipes at my eyes and cheeks.

"Break it. Bomb it. Crush it."

Daddy ignores this. "That was . . . that was some speech you gave, Oliver."

I don't say anything. I keep walking.

"That something you saw on TV? Was that in a movie you saw?"

Again, I don't say anything. The hum of the jets is louder. They're close. I can almost feel the wind of their engines on my back.

"You . . . you didn't win the election, Ollie." My father is a master of understatement. They haven't even voted yet, and I didn't win the election. I've removed even the possibility of plausibly *fixing* the election. "You need to get used to that idea."

I'm used to it. "Pound it. Demolish it. Obliterate it."

"But you should also know something else. Stop walking, Oliver, and look at me."

I stop. He's not pretending to smile or anything stupid like that. "The way you've handled yourself, this whole election. Getting as far as you did . . . a lot of boys wouldn't have the guts to do what you did."

The jets hum like a swarm of approaching locusts.

"I . . . Maybe I was too involved with work to pay enough attention but . . . you did good, son. You did good." And he forcibly grabs me and makes me hug him. He gets down on his knees and presses my head against his bony shoulder.

It would be expensive.

I'd have to arrange for a series of electrical accidents to erase all videotapes of the assembly. I'd have to bribe those FBI agents to leave Mr. Pinckney alone. They must be suspicious by now. I'd have to forge an entire TV show, make it look like it's ten years old, and put a speech in it that's enough like mine that people will believe I just stole it from there. I'd have to fix the television listings so it looks like the fake show was playing the night before the election.

The jets are screaming. Just a few miles away now.

Daddy slaps me on my back. "Heck," he says. "I bet someday we'll look back on this and laugh."

"*Forsan et haec olim meminisse juvabit,*"[118] I mumble.

"What was that?" says Daddy with a furrowed brow. I keep forgetting he took Latin in high school.

"Nothing," I say.

"Come on. Your mom is at home making snickerdoodles." He gives me another hug. "I don't see why we shouldn't celebrate. It takes a lot of courage to run for office, to get up in front of everyone like that. And you . . . Well, I tell you what . . . I'm proud of you." He squeezes me hard. "I'm just so damn proud of you, son."

I pull away and look in his eyes. He means it.

"Cancel that order," I murmur. "Hold your fire. Repeat: Hold your fire. Maybe some other time."

---

118. "Someday we will smile to look back upon even this": Aeneas to his men, after their city had been destroyed by crafty Ulysses, their families killed, and their ships wrecked.

"I didn't hear what you said," says Daddy.

"Nothing important."

He puts his arm around my shoulders and walks me home. Lollipop comes bounding down the street to greet us. Overhead, a flock of black fighter jets screams past us and races for the horizon until they're lost in the blue.